Indigo Nights

Indigo Nights

Heather Graves

ROBERT HALE · LONDON

© Heather Graves 2009
First published in Great Britain 2009

ISBN 978-0-7090-8856-1

Robert Hale Limited
Clerkenwell House
Clerkenwell Green
London EC1R 0HT

www.halebooks.com

2 4 6 8 10 9 7 5 3 1

Typeset in 11½/15½pt New Century Schoolbook
by Derek Doyle & Associates, Shaw Heath
Printed in Great Britain by the MPG Books Group, Bodmin and King's Lynn

PROLOGUE

Paige watched anxiously as her husband finished a conversation on his mobile and snapped it shut, making a fist to punch the air in triumph as he did so. 'Yes!' he said.

'Who was that?' she muttered, although she already knew the answer. She had managed to field all the earlier calls on the land line but this one had turned up on his mobile and slipped through the net.

'Luke Sandford in person – the big man himself! Wants me to ride Black Centurion for him tomorrow at Flemington. And if I can pull it off—'

'Ruary, please!' she interrupted, feeling bound to dampen his enthusiasm. 'I'm not asking, I'm begging you – please don't take that ride.'

He slumped in his chair, squinting at her, his handsome features distorted with irritation. 'Why ever not? It's a great opportunity for me. Sandford has only just returned from a stint in Hong Kong. He's setting up a whole new enterprise here in Victoria—'

'Tell me about it. He's bought a run-down property almost next door to my grandmother. There have already been diggers and bobcats all over the place. He's knocked down the old weatherboard home that had been there for years and is now in the process of building a ranch-style house as well as a stable block with all mod cons.'

'And your grandmother disapproves? Like all old people she's resisting change.'

'And this time I have to agree. It was called Sunny Orchards – a lovely old place. An original Victorian weatherboard, surrounded by apple orchards, plum trees and a market garden.'

Ruary shrugged. 'Times change. I don't suppose they could make a living out of small-time market gardening any more, not these days.'

'Well, Sandford's got his claws on it now. And how long will it be before even that's not enough? Nanou tells me he's planning a private training track as well as a swimming pool for the horses.'

'Good. Strikes me that he's moving into the scene here in earnest. And he'll need a regular rider, won't he? It's an opportunity waiting to be snapped up by someone – why not me?'

'If it were any horse other than Black Centurion. Nanou already warned me never to ride him. He's unpredictable, dangerous.'

'Oh, come on. Since when was I scared of a little danger? It goes hand in hand with the job.'

'Maybe. But why do you think Sandford left it so late to call you? Because everyone else turned him down. Nobody wants that ride.'

'Well, thanks for the vote of confidence,' he said, through gritted teeth. 'The reason he didn't call me personally until now is because you've been taking his messages and not telling me, trying to head him off.'

Caught out, she sighed, knowing the accusation to be true. How many times had she answered the phone to hear that persuasive, upper-class English accent purring in her ear, making her think of the owner as someone who might resemble a very large, feral cat.

Unsure how to explain herself, she stared out of the window at the small square of drought-stricken garden that she hadn't had the time or the energy to do anything about. Married just eighteen months ago in a haze of lust and euphoria, she and Ruary had rented this ground-floor apartment on the understanding that they maintain the front garden. The landlord wouldn't be pleased to see it now.

As if reading her mind, Ruary glanced around at their shabby, secondhand furniture and the dingy apartment, long overdue for a coat of paint.

'If I don't make some serious money soon, we'll never get away from this dismal place. And, anyway, what about you? You haven't been getting the rides lately, have you? Not since we moved to the city. Maybe you should try to find work as a strapper.'

She glanced at him sharply, knowing she would shortly be unfit for too much physical work of any kind. But this wasn't the moment, not while they were bickering, to say that a doctor had told her she was expecting a child. She wouldn't be the first person to try to heal an ailing marriage by introducing a baby. Now she wondered if she was only making things worse.

'You could be right,' she murmured and turned to look into his bright, blue eyes, still sparkling with hostility. All the laughter and fun she had once seen in them – where had it gone? These days they seemed always to be at cross purposes, angry with each other. 'All right, Ruary, let's make a deal. If I call in a few favours and try to find work in a stables, will you give up this ride on Black Centurion?'

'Don't be silly, Paige. No way. If I turn him down now, Luke Sandford will never ask me again and I'll look a prize ass.'

'OK. Let me get this straight. You'd rather face injury – perhaps even death – rather than look a fool?'

'Paige, stop it. You know it's not like that—'

'Isn't it? Nanou told me the history of that horse. He belonged to friends of hers who brought him from New South Wales. He seemed like a bargain at the time but they soon found out why. Black Centurion has changed owners and trainers more than three times, and now somebody's dumped him on Sandford.' Seeing she had her husband's attention at last, she was encouraged to go on. 'He plays up in the starting gates and has already crippled one rider, crushing his legs. He's a rogue animal and he's dangerous.'

'No more than any other spirited horse,' Ruary scoffed. 'And if you think I'm taking advice from your grand-mother. . . .' He made a scornful sound through his teeth.

'Nanou may be old but she knows what she's talking about. She's been around horses all of her life.'

'Well, they're putting blinkers on him tomorrow to keep him focused. And Sandford tells me that when he's focused, he's fast. No one can catch him. So tomorrow, when I come in with the prize money, you'll have to eat your words.'

Paige had only one engagement herself the following day, riding a filly in one of the earlier races. With the main spring carnival over, the Flemington roses were drooping and past their best and, now summer was looming with Christmas not far behind, public interest had turned from racing to cricket and tennis instead. Paige came second in a race that she should have won if only she'd pushed herself harder and given her all. Instead, aware of the new life growing inside her, she had erred on the side of caution and lost the race by a short head. The trainer, who was also an old friend, had been unable to hide her disappointment, lowering Paige's spirits even more.

But now it was time for Ruary's race. It was only 1200 metres – just a quick sprint. She tried to comfort herself with the thought that in less than fifteen minutes it would be over, for better or worse. But nothing could quell the fluttering of nerves in her stomach and her mouth felt dry. She had a bad feeling about this race and it wouldn't go away.

Casually dressed in old jeans and a T-shirt, she left the female changing rooms and strolled out on to the lawn to take up a position near the winning post where she would see the conclusion of the race. Minus her riding boots, helmet and colours, she was anonymous; just another young girl at the track. Without make-up, pale and with fair, curly hair, she knew she looked more like a teenager than a married woman of twenty-two.

She waved to Ruary as he rode from the mounting yard out on to the track, hoping to reassure him of her support, but either he didn't see it or chose to ignore her. In spite of the blinkers, Black Centurion was skittish and hard to control, already fighting the bit and beginning to foam at the mouth. The horse **was** using up precious energy even before the start of the race and she knew it would take all of Ruary's concentration and strength to hold the animal down and keep him calm until the barriers opened and the race was under way.

It was a field of some fifteen horses, some with little experience other than track work and largely untried. Only Black Centurion had any reputation and that wasn't good. She covered her eyes with her hand and squinted into the distance, trying to see what was happening as jockey after jockey had to dismount behind the barriers, allowing the attendants to wrestle each horse into its appointed place. Black Centurion was one of the first to go in, kicking out viciously and fighting them all the way. Once he was safe in the stalls, Ruary climbed back into the saddle, hoping one of the attendants would stay to help him restrain the big black horse.

Unfortunately, before they could come under the starter's orders, another horse took fright and bucked in the stalls, ending up lying flat on the ground. All the attendants had to rush forward to unfasten the gate and help get him out.

Black Centurion, frightened by the drama that he couldn't see, also reared in the barriers and caught himself on a piece of television equipment which shouldn't have been there. The skin of his neck tore open as if someone had undone a zipper and the horse, maddened by fright and the pain of his injury, forced his way through the barriers and bolted off down the track towards the finishing post. He was fired up and Ruary had no chance of controlling him. One of the clerks of the course took off in pursuit but Black Centurion had no intention of being caught. He dodged the man's clutching fingers and missed his footing, crashing into the inside barrier and tossing Ruary high in the air before taking off again, riderless and at full tilt. Ruary fell awkwardly like a rag doll and lay motionless on the track. Paramedics dashed towards him while the clerk took off in pursuit of the rogue horse.

Paige, too appalled to scream, crossed the track and hurried on trembling legs towards the paramedics who had put Ruary in a neck brace and were already lifting him on to a stretcher prior to getting him into the ambulance.

10

'Stand aside, miss,' One of the paramedics moved to stop her climbing into the ambulance to be with him.

'Please – I'm his wife,' she explained. The two men glanced at each other and shrugged, one of them quickly adjusting an oxygen mask on Ruary's face.

'How is he?' she whispered. 'Is it very bad?' The paramedics exchanged glances again and one of them nodded, unsmiling.

'Unconscious but still alive. Just,' he said as the ambulance trundled from the course and took off at speed, sirens blaring, when they reached the highway.

On arrival at the hospital, routine took over and Ruary was whisked from view while Paige had to give his personal details to a nurse. After this, she was shown to a waiting-room with a set of uncomfortable chairs and television overhead, showing a children's programme, the bobbing puppets with their inane chatter rasping her nerves. There was also a coffee table covered with old and well-thumbed magazines. Paige tried not to think of the germs they must harbour. Several people were sitting around looking tired and bored as if they had already been there far too long.

Sitting alone and with nothing to do, she knew she ought to call Ruary's mother but couldn't yet summon the strength to do so. Lyddie McHugh was a widow with a nervous and querulous disposition. Ruary had always been the light of her life and Paige didn't want to alert her until she had something positive to report. Whatever the outcome of this accident, Ruary wouldn't be an easy patient.

The door of the emergency ward opened and an anxious-looking young doctor came into the room, carrying a clipboard. All eyes turned towards him expectantly until he called out, 'Mrs McHugh? Paige McHugh?'

'That's me,' she said, standing up and feeling suddenly breathless. 'Can I see my husband now? Is he all right?'

'Please.' The young doctor didn't look any happier as he addressed himself to her. 'Come into the office where we can talk in private.'

'But Ruary will be all right?' She felt a chill down her spine. 'Not going to be crippled or anything?'

The doctor looked even more uncomfortable as he ushered Paige into a small consulting-room and sat her down in a chair beside him before he spoke.

'Mrs Paige – Mrs McHugh – we did all we could but we lost him. I'm so sorry, but I have to tell you your husband is dead.'

For a moment Paige felt dizzy and the room seemed to lurch. She was grateful that she was already sitting down. She closed her eyes, waiting for the vertigo to pass.

'I really am sorry.' The doctor seemed genuinely upset himself. 'Death is always a shock – especially when it isn't expected.'

Not expected! Paige almost wanted to laugh, but she knew he would think her hysterical. She had been expecting the worst ever since Ruary agreed to ride Black Centurion. Needing someone to blame, she thought of Luke Sandford, silently cursing him for his persistence.

The doctor was speaking again. 'Is there anyone you'd like us to call for you? Any relative? You shouldn't be coping with this alone.'

'Just . . . give me a moment.' Paige shook her head, fighting to clear it. How could this happen? How could Ruary be dead? Ruary who just a few hours ago had been full of life and vitality, scoffing at danger. So she might have fallen out of love with him as he had with her, but that didn't mean there was no care between them. And when the baby came, they'd be a family again. Or so she had thought. But now all those dreams had been shattered and she was facing the future alone as a single parent. As neither she nor Ruary had any siblings, they didn't have much of an extended family – she had Nanou, her grandmother and he had his mother, Lyddie.

Thinking of Lyddie brought her down to earth with a jolt and she opened her eyes to look into the doctor's anxious gaze. She hadn't been able to face the thought of talking to Lyddie before but with Ruary dead it was going to be ten times worse.

A nurse knocked and poked her head around the door. 'Excuse me, Doctor Scott but there's a gentleman here asking after Mr McHugh and I wondered . . .'

'Is he a relative?'

'A close friend – so he says.'

The doctor glanced at Paige who shrugged, nodding assent. She couldn't think who it might be but any friendly face would be welcome at this stage.

'Thank you, Nurse. Please send him in.' Doctor Scott's expression cleared. Here was a lifeline, someone to help him deal with Mrs McHugh and her loss. A young house physician, not yet case hardened, he was unused to breaking bad news and was visibly relieved at the prospect of passing responsibility for the young widow to somebody else.

Paige looked up and frowned, not recognizing the tall, undeniably handsome man who came in, dominating the small room with his presence. Dressed in an expensive dark blue suit and carrying a hat, she knew at once that he had come directly from the track. His skin was naturally tanned but not excessively and he had dark, springy hair that stood up in a quiff at the front. He smiled reassuringly at Paige and at the doctor, clearly unaware of the tragedy that had occurred. Paige had no idea who he was until he introduced himself and she recognized his voice.

'Luke Sandford,' he said. 'So sorry about the accident. I got here as soon as I could.'

Paige drew herself up and took a deep breath, feeling colour rush to her cheeks. 'Sorry are you? Sorry for hounding my husband to ride your dangerous horse?'

'Excuse me?' Sandford looked at Paige a little less kindly now. 'But I haven't hounded anyone. I'm very sorry about Ruary's accident, but I didn't cause it. Blame the television company for putting that piece of equipment on his gate. I'm thinking of suing them. It wasn't much fun for me, either, you know. My horse wounded and bolting like that. But Ruary's an experienced rider – he knew the risks and was prepared to take them.' He looked from the doctor to Paige and back again, becoming uncomfortably aware of their grim expressions. 'He is going to be all right, isn't he? Few broken bones, eh? Nothing a stint in plaster won't fix? Oh and don't you worry about his medical expenses, Mrs McHugh. I'll arrange with the hospital to pay any bills.'

Paige could bear it no longer and rose to her feet, the better to meet Luke Sandford's cool, enquiring gaze. 'There aren't going to be any bills, Mr Sandford, apart from the funeral expenses,' she said. 'My husband is dead.'

CHAPTER ONE

Paige had spent the happiest days of her life in her grandmother's house. As a child, with parents too busy travelling
to provide a permanent home for her, she had grown up
there, the old homestead being a part of her security for as
long as she could remember. And when her parents failed
to return from a complicated aid mission to Africa that had
gone horribly wrong, she continued to live there with
Nanou until she married.

The homestead was solid and built to last with walls of
the local granite – thick walls that helped to keep it cooler
in summer and cosy in winter, repelling the southerly
winds that seemed to drive across the Southern Ocean
straight from the South Pole. The furniture was solid and
old-fashioned, built to last and the curtains, although old
and faded now, had been of the best imported silk brocade
when Nanou had installed them. It was a spacious home,
built to accommodate guests although they didn't have
many these days. And she had always loved to see her
grandmother's influence on what had been an original
pioneer homestead; her provincial French kitchen with its
old-fashioned deep sinks, walk in pantries and cupboards
that could hold so much more than their modern equivalent.

Loops of garlic and bunches of dried herbs hung from the rafters, giving off an aroma of lavender, exotic spices and the promise of good food. It was always a happy place, full of light and air.

Outside, a tree-lined drive connected the homestead with the main road. In a circular garden, set in the large lawn outside the front door and where they could enjoy the most sun and protection from wind were her grandmother's roses. The soil had been turned over and enriched, prior to planting, and the roses rewarded her with a fantastic show. She favoured the sweet-smelling, old fashioned varieties, particularly those of French origin – fat and flamboyant – many-petalled roses that didn't know when to stop blooming. Only when winter set in for good at the end of June did she have the heart to prune them. The only rose at the back of the house was a sturdy Pierre de Ronsard that had been there for more years than anyone cared to remember. Surrounding the back door it was escaping up the wall, trying to follow the sun. Behind the homestead were a series of fenced paddocks not often used for horses now and mostly falling into neglect. There was also a large stable block opposite the back of the house.

Paige felt right at home in the stables, the original dozen or so stalls, having been renovated and extended by her grandfather who had kept race horses as well as breeding and raising the occasional foal. Of course, in his day the stables had been alive with activity, every stall occupied and swarming with lads and strappers going about their routine tasks of walking, grooming the animals and keeping them clean. The decline happened only after his death – an event that Paige didn't remember as it happened before she was born. Nanou told her he had been a man who loved to live life to the full.

'I'm here for a good time, not a long time,' he told his wife, paying scant attention to his doctors who told him to quit smoking and give up the brandy he liked to drink in the evening. Unfortunately, their predictions turned out to be true. His old tantalus stood on the sideboard in the dining-room. It still contained liquor but it was locked and no one could find the key.

Nowadays the stables were almost empty but not quite. Her grandmother had been a keen horsewoman, too and she liked to keep her hand in with training up the occasional promising horse. Usually, she would get impatient and sell it long before it had the chance to bring her the fame and fortune she deserved.

Situated on the Mornington Peninsula behind Frankston and Mornington, not too close nor too far from the sea, the homestead was in an ideal position; a country property yet still within easy reach of the city. Over the years, more than one developer had cast envious eyes on land in such a prime position, hoping to make her an offer she couldn't refuse, but Paige Warrender – whose mind was still as sharp as that of the granddaughter who had been named for her – steadfastly refused to part with so much as a single paddock of her now very valuable land.

'This estate has been in my husband's family for three generations,' she boasted. 'And he wouldn't expect me to sell it just because he's no longer here. The last thing he would want is to see his paddocks covered with ugly town houses all crowded together and looking the same. If I were to part with so much as a blade of grass for that purpose, he would turn in his grave.'

'But, Mrs Warrender, you must know you're sitting on a gold mine here?'

'Am I?' She shrugged. '*Bon.*'

'And surely a big place like this is too much for you now that you're getting on in—'

'Hold it right there.' She would fix them with a steely glint in her eye. 'Don't you know it's an insult to tell a Frenchwoman she's getting old?'

She would go on to tell them the story of how Frank Warrender had brought her to the peninsula some forty years ago as a bride and the businessmen would fold their arms and pretend to listen, fencing around the subject a little longer. But the end result was always the same: they went away empty-handed.

So it was to this house, simply called *Warrender* – her grandfather's family name – that Paige retreated five years ago in her hour of grief and need. And here she had remained. Sometimes, she wondered where those five years had gone, finding it hard to believe it was really that long since Ruary had been killed. But her lively little son, Marc, was there to remind her of the passage of time, no longer a baby but running everywhere on sturdy, little-boy legs. And there was Nanou, of course, the grandmother she adored and who had welcomed her back without ever asking how long she would stay.

Unlike most girl jockeys who tend to give up riding professionally after marriage and childbirth, Paige had been eager to return to the track, although with the advent of new and promising apprentices each year and living so far from the city race tracks, she didn't get many rides. But she kept her hand in by riding track work for her grand-mother. Slender and strong as ever, at first glance she still looked more like a teenager than a young mother approaching thirty.

Nanou's most promising horse at the moment was a four-year-old mare who had won convincingly on the provincial courses and had recently done well in the city. A bay, going by the old-fashioned name of Pierette, she had been born here at Warrender, almost the last of her grandfather's good bloodlines. As Pierette had been slow to develop and show her potential, Nanou had been on the point of selling her more than once until Paige reminded her that her impatience had cost her money before. Begging the old lady to persevere just a little longer, Paige told her she had a good feeling about the horse. And, as she matured, Pierette was proving to be one of those rare female horses with an unusually aggressive nature and a will to win and, as she grew in both age and stamina, the longer races suited her best. This morning's work at the local track had been especially promising and, returning to the homestead, Paige was looking forward to telling her grandmother that their patience was about to be rewarded.

Her smile faded when she saw Nanou seated at the kitchen table, frowning behind her spectacles and opening bills.

'Too early for that, Nanou,' she teased. 'Get some breakfast into you first.'

Her grandmother huffed, refusing to be cheered. 'Look at this. Soon as Christmas is over, the bills come rolling in. The rates have gone up again. And where I'm to find the money this time, I've no idea—'

'They'll let you pay in instalments, won't they?' Paige poured herself coffee, refusing to sink into her grandmother's gloom. 'Anyway, something always turns up.'

'Does it?' Her grandmother seemed unconvinced.

'This isn't like you, Nanou, to be so despondent.'

'I know. Maybe I *am* getting old, like the man said.'

'Not you. Forget the bills for a moment and listen. I'm starting to get a really good feeling about Pierette. She

19

seems to work stronger every day and she tries, really tries to beat everyone else, even at track work. I know it's too early to say but she really might be good enough to make it to the Melbourne Cup.' And Paige sat back, grinning, wondering why Nanou didn't show more enthusiasm for this latest news.

'Pierette. Um – yes.' She looked away, unwilling to meet her granddaughter's gaze. 'I've been meaning to talk to you about that.'

Paige's shoulders slumped. 'I know that look. Come on, Nanou, out with it. What have you done?'

'What I should have done a long time ago. I'm selling Pierette.'

'Oh, no. Not just as all our hard work is about to pay off. Why didn't you tell me things were that bad? I still have some of Ruary's insurance money left.'

'No, I can't take your money, Paige. You'll need every penny of it for yourself and little Marc. What about his education?'

'He'll do all right at a state school. I did.'

'Hmm.' Nanou gave her a sideways glance. This was an old bone of contention between them. Paige had played truant from about the age of fourteen and had left school as soon as she could to become a jockey.

'All right, I'll make some extra money. I'll take on track work for somebody else – push a little harder to get more rides.'

'Paige—'

'No, you listen to me. If we sell Pierette, what are we going to do next time the bills come rolling in? We'll have no hope at all and nothing to bargain with.'

'All right then, I must tell you. I can see you'll give me no peace till I do. It's not just Pierette I'm thinking of selling

20

– it's everything. Trying to hang on to Warrender is foolish – it's only putting off the inevitable. How are you ever going to afford to keep it when I die?'

Paige felt a small shiver of panic. 'I hate it when you talk about dying. You're not even old.'

'Oh, I am. But you don't wish to see it. I'll be seventy-three next year.'

'Rubbish. Seventy is the new fifty.' She was struck by a horrible thought. 'You're not sick, are you?'

'Of course not. I'm never sick. I just think we should be practical and look to the future, that's all.'

'Well, I don't want to. I'd rather live in the present.'

'An' bury your 'ead in the sand like the emu?'

'Ostrich.'

'Same thing.' The old lady gave one of her Gallic shrugs.

'Oh, Nanou, it isn't the same thing at all.' Paige giggled. 'I do love you so much. You always make me laugh.'

But her grandmother still wasn't smiling. 'Paige, we must face it. I don't see any way out of it. I 'ave to sell *Warrender*, lock stock and barrel.'

Paige slumped into a chair and stared back at her, wondering if the old lady really was starting to lose her mind.

'And there's no need to look like that,' Nanou said, accurately reading her thoughts. 'I'm not crazy. Come to my senses, more like.'

'Nanou, you mustn't do this.' Paige spoke in a broken whisper, her mouth suddenly dry. 'You've always said Granpa would turn in his grave if—'

'And so he would if I were to sell out to a developer. But I'm not. The offer has come from another horseman – someone like you and me. Someone who wants to bring it all back to life and realize its full potential. Someone who has money enough to do it.'

Paige almost snorted. 'That sounds like businessman-speak to me.'

'When was the last time you looked at this place? Really looked at it? Picturesque? Yes. But neglected – a property run into the ground. The plumbing is old and we'll need a new water-heater soon – this one's only going on a wing and a prayer. The roof leaks when there's a storm, the whole place needs re-wiring and – need I go on? It needs thousands and I just can't afford it.'

'These are details, Nanou.' Paige waved towards a cupboard containing some china they never used. 'Surely, we can sell some of those antiques and buy a new water-heater?'

'That service is Limoges. It belonged to my mother.' The old lady's lips set in sullen lines. 'I brought it from France.'

'Oh? And what's the good of a fancy dinner service if you don't have a cupboard to keep it in?' Paige knew she was being cruel but she was desperate to get her point across. 'And if you can't think clearly about your own future or mine, what about Marc? You've always said he will inherit all this.'

'Marc is a baby. It will be fifteen – twenty years before he knows his own mind. He might be a city boy and want nothing to do with life in the country.'

'Where did you get that idea? You've only to look at him to know that he loves it here as much as I do. It's the only home he has ever known.'

There was silence for a moment and to Paige's horror, the old lady's face crumpled and she began to weep silently, huge tears splashing unheeded on to her gnarled hands. Nanou never cried and this was the first time Paige had seen it. Filled with remorse, she rushed to embrace her,

22

comforting her as if she were Marc.

'Oh, Nanou, I'm sorry, so sorry. It's not your fault. You've been wonderful and we must have been such a burden, Marc and me.'

'A burden, yes.' She didn't deny it as she sniffed, drying her tears on a dishcloth. 'But one I was 'appy to carry as long as I could.'

'Well, you're not to worry about anything any more. I'm taking over responsibility now. I'll work hard and somehow we'll find the money for the water-heater and the re-wiring.'

'Oh, Paige, you can't. It's too much—'

'Of course it isn't. I'd no idea things were so desperate – you should have said.' Suddenly, she was struck by a disquieting thought. 'How far have you gone with it – this sale of the property? I hope it isn't too late to back out?'

'I don't know. I haven't signed any contracts yet, if that's what you mean. So far it's just talk – a promise to consider the offer and take it further – but. . . .'

'Well, if they're business people, I'm sure they've been disappointed before. And there must be other properties for sale on the peninsula.'

'Not like this one – already next door to their own.' The old lady could scarcely meet her granddaughter's searching gaze. 'I know you won't like this, Paige, but our prospective buyer is our newest neighbour – Luke Sandford.'

'Well, of course it is.' Paige felt a rush of temper as she stood up and grabbed her handbag and car keys from the sideboard. 'I should've guessed he'd want to start expand-ing his empire. I'm only surprised it's taken him so long. Nanou, will you collect Marc from play school if I'm not back by twelve?'

'Yes, but where are you going?'

'Where do you think? To pay a visit next door. It's time I told Mr Luke Sandford a few home truths.'

'Now, Paige! Paige!' Her grandmother called after her, but the girl was already gone, running towards her old Holden Commodore. 'Don't do anything rash.'

Luke Sandford was having a bad morning. The stock market was down, wiping thousands of dollars off his investment shares. And now Lisa, his personal assistant, who had been his reliable right hand for the last ten years, was leaving to marry a film producer and going to live in L.A.

He decided there was little to be gained by remaining in town, where he was liable to lose his temper and say unkind things to Lisa who was, after all, free to leave whenever she chose. It wasn't her fault that he had taken her so for granted, relying on her as a permanent fixture in his life. They had suited each other so well, the relationship always professional, friendly but never flirtatious. He didn't look forward to choosing and dealing with somebody new. There! Lisa had given her notice only this morning and he was already thinking of her in the past tense. But the film producer was good-looking, young and madly in love with her, so it was unlikely that she would change her mind.

His mobile rang just as he was getting into his Porsche and he saw it was his stable foreman from Sunny Orchards. He had kept the rather twee name of the old homestead he had rebuilt, never having got round to changing it.

'Yes, Tom?'

'There's a young lady here to see you.' The foreman lowered his voice, indicating that she might not be too far away. 'I said you were at your office in town but she—'

'No. I'm actually on my way down to you. Did she give a name?'

'Seemed a bit riled up when I said you weren't here. Says she's acting on behalf of Mrs Warrender from next door.'

'Oh, good.' Luke's spirits rose for the first time that day. 'Looks like she's made up her mind to sell and sent someone round to thrash out the details. Give the lady some coffee and get her to wait – I'll be there within the hour.'

'Wait a minute, Luke.' Tom started to say. 'I don't really think it's—'

But his employer had already rung off.

By the time Luke arrived, some forty minutes later, Paige was still angry but her initial rush of temper had somewhat abated. She was seated in a comfortable armchair, a coffee table beside her well stocked with horse-breeding glossies as well as magazines reviewing the latest in sports cars. She found that irritating, too. Why was it, she thought miserably, that people like Luke Sandford could afford any boys' toys they wanted, while she and her grandmother had such a struggle simply to live?

She heard the Porsche arriving and took a deep breath. Over the past three-quarters of an hour, she had imagined herself saying all kinds of clever, hurtful things but now the moment had come, she decided to state her case, telling him simply that *Warrender* was not, and never would be, for sale.

And, although she hadn't seen him since that day at the hospital, she recognized him immediately when he came in. At first glance she could see little change in him except that his dark hair was beginning to be sprinkled with grey. He was tanned as before and was conventionally dressed in

25

another immaculate dark-blue suit over a white shirt. But on looking more closely, she could see there was a subtle difference in his manner; a look of sadness and vulnerability in his dark-brown eyes. Purple shadows beneath them betrayed a lack of sleep. A lot of the bounce that had once so annoyed her was gone and somehow he no longer looked like the man who had everything. Something bad must have happened to make him look so lost.

She pulled herself out of these thoughts. This was not why she was here. She wasn't here to feel sorry for Luke Sandford whose new vulnerability made him so much more likeable. Irrationally, she caught herself wishing she had taken more trouble with her own appearance but she had run out of the house in her old riding clothes straight from track work, no make-up and her fair hair scragged back in an unkempt pony-tail.

At first sight of her, Luke felt a small flash of irritation himself. This was no law clerk come to talk of property and conveyancing. This girl looked more like a strapper in search of a job; someone Tom could have dealt with himself in five minutes. But there was something about that determined little face that was strangely familiar. He couldn't place her at this very moment but he was certain he would. Luke Sandford never forgot a face.

'How can I help you?' he said. 'If you're looking for work, that isn't my bag. My foreman deals with any vacancies in the stables.'

'No, Mr Sandford, I'm not looking for work.' She gave a wry smile, remembering how she had rushed out of the house with no thought for the impression that she might make. 'But I can see how you might think that. No. I have come on behalf of my grandmother, Mrs Warrender.'

Luke snapped his fingers. 'I know you now. You're Mrs

26

McHugh. I remembered the face as soon as I heard the voice. So you're Mrs Warrender's granddaughter – I had no idea.'

'Clearly not. Had you known you would be dealing with me rather than with a frail old lady—'

'Excuse me, but from what I know of your grandmother, she didn't strike me as being in the least bit frail.'

'That's as may be. But for the last five years – on and off – she has been beseiged by pests trying to get her to part with some or all of her land. She has been struggling to keep the property together and—'

'Exactly. That's what she told me herself, explaining that this is why the place is so run down.'

'I see. You expect to acquire it cheaply because a few minor things are in need of repair?'

He sat back, regarding her, shaking his head. 'I don't know what I've ever done that you should have such a bad opinion of me, Mrs McHugh, but I'd like to alter it if I can. I'm not a bad man or a greedy one, in spite of what you seem to think. If you still bear me a grudge for what happened to your husband, I do understand. It's hard to move on from something like that.'

'Yes. Yes, it is,' Paige murmured although, even as she said it, she realized it wasn't quite true. Five years on, she could see that her marriage to Ruary wouldn't have gone the distance. She found out only after he died that he'd had more than one secret lover. One even came to his funeral dressed in deepest mourning like a Victorian widow, complete with black handkerchiefs and black veils. Only the quick action of the funeral director had prevented her from casting herself into the grave with the coffin and making a scene. Finding out about Ruary's women couldn't help but alter Paige's perspective and it was only when

Marc reminded her with an expression that was entirely his father's that she gave a thought to her dead husband at all. Luke misinterpreted her thoughtfulness for remembered sorrow and sighed.

'I don't know about you,' he said at last, 'but I missed breakfast today and I'm starved. Would you care to join me for an early lunch?'

Paige opened her mouth to refuse but her stomach betrayed her, growling at the mention of food.

'Sounds as if you didn't have breakfast either.' He smiled. 'I know of a nice little bistro just down the road.'

Paige glanced down at her riding clothes still smelling vaguely of horse's sweat. 'Mr Sandford, I came here straight from the stables. I'm hardly dressed for smart company—'

'It isn't. I promise you, it's only a pub. And call me Luke, please. Mr Sandford always makes me think of my father.'

'Then you must call me Paige.'

'Paige,' he said, almost savouring it. 'I like that. Unusual.'

'French. It's my grandmother's name as well, but I always call her Nanou,' she said, forcing herself to remember the real purpose of this visit.

'We'll take my car. I'll drop you back here afterwards to pick up your own.'

As Paige got into the silver Porsche that smelled of his very expensive aftershave and good leather, she asked herself what she was doing. She had come to Sunny Orchards ready to blow Luke Sandford out of the water and yet here she was getting into his car and allowing him to take her to lunch.

Much as she expected, he drove fast and competently, giving all his attention to the road. In less than ten

28

minutes, they were drawing into the car-park of a pretty, old-fashioned hotel overlooking the beach.

'And you say it isn't smart,' she said ruefully, trying to slap dust off her riding breeches.

'All right. To keep you company, I'll take off my jacket,' he said. 'And we'll eat outside on the veranda. Catch a better view of the sea.'

'You like the sea, Luke?'

'Yeah.' He gave her a real smile that completely lit up his face. 'Spent every moment I could on a surfboard when I was a kid. That's when I wasn't on the back of a horse.'

'You ride?' she said, surprised by this piece of news.

'You're surprised? I wasn't always this big, fat business-man in a suit.'

She studied him yet again. He was tall, yes, and broad-shouldered, but there wasn't an ounce of fat on his slender but muscular figure. He must be well into his forties but he looked fit as a man half his age, as if he worked out.

'Oh, you're not. I didn't mean . . .'

'It's all right.' He smiled ruefully. 'I must seem middle-aged to you. Very staid.'

'Not really,' she said. 'How old do you think *I* am.'

'That's a dangerous question – I could be in trouble here.' He laughed. 'But I'll stick my neck out and say you don't look a day over twenty-four.'

'Give or take a month or so, I'm nearly twenty-eight.'

'Whew,' he said, pretending to be relieved. 'I came through that one OK. Now what are you going to eat? I can recommend the poached salmon with chips and salad. Hungry people need good, plain food.'

'Thank you,' she said. 'That sounds wonderful.'

She visited the Ladies while he ordered the food, hoping to do something to improve her appearance. She washed a

smut off her nose, found a comb in her bag and undid the
pony-tail, trying to civilize her hair. Loose, it made a disor-
derly halo of ash-blonde curls but somehow it seemed a
little less severe. She considered lipstick and decided
against it, not wanting him to think she was trying too
hard. She returned to the table to find him seated with a
champagne bottle in an ice bucket rather than the regular
lunchtime single glass. He poured it for her before she
could say she didn't usually drink in the daytime but she
bit back the words, not wanting to sound prissy.

Of course, on an empty stomach, just a couple of sips
went straight to her head and she set the glass down carefully, pushing it away.

'You don't like it?' he said, seeing the gesture. 'I'll get you
something else.'

'No. It's lovely. But I really should have a glass of water
before drinking any more.'

He summoned a waitress who hurried to bring them a
jug of iced water. Luke Sandford seemed to be well known
and liked here.

Their meal arrived shortly afterwards and they attacked
it with murmurs of pleasure. The pub specialized in
seafood and the salmon was cooked to perfection in a light,
lemon-flavoured sauce, the chips hot and crisp and the
salad of mixed greens, crisp and fresh. They didn't say very
much until they had finished and the debris had been
cleared away when they returned their attention to the
champagne.

'It seems such a waste,' she said. 'We can't drink it all as
we're driving.'

'Doesn't matter,' he said. 'Would you like something
more? Or just coffee to finish?'

'Coffee, please,' she said, still looking at the unfinished

bottle of champagne. 'Would it be awfully rude,' she said, 'to ask them to re-cork it somehow and let me take it home to Nanou? She loves champagne and we don't have it often.'

Luke didn't seem to mind this at all and was quick to arrange it. Then he sat back, regarding her across the table. 'Can we talk business now?'

Oh dear, here comes the crunch, she thought, having let herself hope for a moment that he wasn't going to raise the subject of business, after all. But, of course, that's why he had brought her here – not because he had any interest in her but to soften her up.

She took a deep breath and drew herself up.

'Luke, I'm sorry you've wasted your time and your money on me, but I don't really think we have anything to discuss. *Warrender* isn't for sale – or ever likely to be – it's my son's inheritance, his future.'

'You have a son?' This news seemed to astonish him. 'I talked to Mrs Warrender for some time and she never said anything about—'

'And, as I recall, she didn't tell you anything about me, either. She's been a widow a long time, you know – used to making all these decisions on her own.'

'And how old is your son now?'

'Marc is almost five. I was already expecting him when Ruary died.'

'Oh.' He put his hand over his mouth, regarding her with something between pain and nostalgia in his gaze. 'I remember my own son at that age. Everything in the world is a source of wonder and magic; even the simplest thing like a butterfly pausing to drink from a flower.'

'And how old is your boy now?' she said, expecting him to act the proud father and tell of a boy in college or already part of his father's business empire.

Instead Luke stared down at his coffee cup, as if it were painful to say anything at all. 'Alan would have been twenty-four this year.'

'Would have been?'

'He's dead. Another soldier, killed by a car bomb in Afghanistan. Just a statistic now.'

'I'm so sorry,' she whispered. 'It must have been awful for you – and for your wife.'

'It was a bad time. In many ways, it still is. My wife, Rachel, got through it by being angry – with the army, with the government for sending him there – but mostly with me. We were divorced last year.'

Vaguely, Paige could remember a news item of good-looking young men in uniform killed overseas but she wasn't one for watching the television news.

Making an effort to control his emotions and succeeding, Luke straightened his shoulders and sighed. 'But I didn't bring you here to talk of my woes. I hoped we could reach a compromise – something to benefit all of us.'

'Now if this is a roundabout way of trying to get us to sell—'

'Not at all. I can see that is out of the question now. But, may I ask how much use you are making of those very fine stables Mrs Warrender showed me? Far as I could see, you have only one horse.'

'Yes, and a good one – Pierette We don't want to sell her, either.'

To her surprise, he laughed. 'Will you stop jumping down my throat until you hear what I have to say. While we were chatting, I've had time to think. It's the use of your paddocks and stables that I really need. What if I were to lease them from your grandmother – oh, and I'd pay you to ride track work for me, as well?'

CHAPTER TWO

She didn't get back home until after four, to find Nanou and Marc sitting at the kitchen table having afternoon tea. Nanou gave her a quizzical look while Marc grinned up at her with cake crumbs on his chin and a moustache of milk above his mouth.

'Mummee!' he yelled, getting up and hurling himself into her arms. Deftly, she wiped away most of the milk before receiving a smacking kiss. 'Where've you been? You've been gone all day.'

'Well?' Nanou regarded her, head on one side. 'It's a fair question, Paige. Have you eaten? As I recall you flew out of here in a temper without any breakfast.'

'Yes,' Paige said, dropping a kiss on her son's head before releasing him. 'I have, as a matter of fact. Luke Sandford took me to lunch.'

'Lunch?' Nanou's eyes widened in surprise. 'You were in such a rage when you left here, I thought you were going to roast the man over a slow fire rather than let him take you to lunch.'

'It was no big deal, only the pub.' Paige shrugged, trying to play it down.

'But dressed like that and smelling of sweat and the stables?'

Paige laughed. 'Oh, Nanou, you can be so old-fashioned sometimes. Nobody cares so much about appearance these days.'

'That's what you modern girls like to think. But men are simple creatures and I don't think they've changed all that much over the years. They still like to see a woman look well turned out.'

'Nanou, I went to talk business with him, not to seduce him.' Paige raised her eyes heavenwards. All the same she felt a tell-tale flush of colour suffusing her cheeks. It *had* crossed her mind to wonder what it might be like to make love with Luke Sandford. For the past five years she had devoted herself to her baby son and there had been no room for a man in her life. Somehow Luke Sandford had stirred up feelings she had considered long buried, or dead, and she wasn't sure how to handle them. So she decided to crush and ignore them instead.

'Aha,' Knowing her granddaughter so well, the old lady was quick to pick up on her mood. 'He charmed you, didn't he? Or you wouldn't 'ave taken so long to get home. So tell me, what conclusions did you and the toothsome Mr Sandford reach?'

'Toothsome now, is it? Really, Nanou, for an old lady you pay far too much attention to men.'

'And you don't pay enough,' the old lady retorted, her nostrils flaring slightly as she gave Paige a superior smile. 'I am after all a Frenchwoman. We never stop being interested in men.'

'I'm all right as I am.'

'That's because no one has reached you yet – roused your passions.'

'I've been married, haven't I? And I have a son.'

'So? Victorian women could produce a throng of children

without feeling the smallest stirring of lust. The best thing Ruary ever did was to give you Marc. Let's leave it at that.'

'Gladly.' Paige deliberately misunderstood although she knew her grandmother was by no means finished with the subject of love and romance.

'You are like the sleeping beauty – a little caterpillar living inside a comfortable cocoon. One day you will look up and set eyes on a man. Your knees will tremble, your heart will feel as if it has turned in your breast. He will meet your gaze and walk across a roomful of people to meet you. He will know, just as you do, that you have found "the one". You won't be able to breathe, let alone speak and once you have kissed, the future is sealed for both of you—'

'Love at first sight, Nanou? Really!' Paige was starting to giggle.

'Laugh all you like, but one day it will happen and you'll have to believe me.' Once in the full flow of her narrative, Nanou was not to be halted. 'Nights of passion will follow. Indigo nights that seem never-ending, yet pass in an instant; hours flying by as if they were minutes—'

'Nanou,' Paige said softly, no longer laughing, 'are you telling me that's how it was with you and Grandpa?'

'Oh, yes.' The old lady's eyes softened as she remembered. 'I was twenty-six – on the way to being an old maid in those days – and he was well over forty. But that didn't matter. He was the love of my life.'

About the same age difference as Luke and me! The thought came into Paige's mind. Immediately, she crushed it with a tart remark.

'So you were fortunate that he was a man of substance. I don't suppose you were allowed to meet anyone who wasn't.'

Nanou laughed. 'I would have loved that sunburned

Australian if he'd been a penniless swagman. And it was the fifties, you know, not the Victorian era. People celebrating after the terrifying years of war. Everyone travelled and nobody came to Europe without visiting Paris.'

'So that's where you met Grandpa – in Paris?'

'I did indeed. And it was love at first sight for both of us. But it wasn't easy – my parents tried to put obstacles in our path. They didn't want me to marry and live on the other side of the world, but they changed their tune when I told them I was pregnant with your father. Your grandfather brought me here to *Warrender* and I never thought of living anywhere else. The rest you know.'

'No wonder it breaks your heart to think of parting with it.'

The old lady shrugged. 'Sentiment won't put food in our bellies. So tell me, what did you and Mr Sandford decide?'

'Nothing, of course, without talking it over with you. But he did make an interesting proposition and we may be able to reach a compromise.' Briefly, she outlined Luke's offer to lease their empty stables and employ Paige to ride track work for him at the same time. He had even offered to let Paige exercise Pierette on his private track and make use of the horses' swimming pool.

'I find that hard to believe,' her grandmother said when she finished. 'It all sounds too good to be true.' She thought about it for a moment. 'He must realize what he's doing, I suppose? If he leases the stables from me and provides you with paid work, he's giving us the very means to hold out against him, refusing to sell. Why would he do that?'

'Because he told me his real need was for the extra stable space and the use of our paddocks.'

'Yes but that's only half the truth. Did he tell you anything about his domestic arrangements? His family?'

'It's a sad story. His wife divorced him soon after their son was killed in Afghanistan. I was telling him about Marc and he reminisced about his own son at that age. It got quite sentimental.'

'No doubt. But did he tell you about his new fiancée?'

'No.' Once again Paige felt a blush rising from her throat. 'Is there any reason that he should?'

Nanou stared out of the window, looking thoughtful. 'Well, he told me that was the main reason for wanting this place. To renovate it and convert it into a palace fit for his new bride.'

'No,' Paige said slowly. 'But at the time he thought he was dealing with you on your own. Until I went over there, he knew nothing of Marc or of me.' She considered this for a moment. 'But, Nanou, when he came to the house, he must have seen a child's belongings about the place?'

'He wouldn't think anything of it. Lots of grandmothers keep clothing and toys for visiting grandchildren.'

'All the same, he wasn't entirely honest with me. Maybe leasing the stables is just his way of getting his foot in the door. Maybe we should refuse.'

'Now, Paige, don't let's jump to conclusions. Leasing those empty stables to Sandford will benefit all of us. We should take his offer at face value and leave it at that.' She laughed shortly. 'His fiancée might even turn her nose up at our old-fashioned house. And the distance from the city.'

'Which isn't as far as it was now we have the new motorways,' Paige murmured, trying not to sound too interested. 'So who is she? Did he say?'

'Julia Canning. The events organizer. You must have heard of her?'

'Yes, I have.' Paige pulled a wry face. 'I was at school with Sarah, her younger sister. Always bragging that Julia could

37

get free tickets for all the best concerts.'

'But you weren't one of her clique?'

'For a while I was. We had the same cruel sense of humour as teenagers do. For a while we were almost best friends. She even came to barbecue here – my birthday party, I think. Vaguely, I can remember Julia coming to pick her up in somebody's sports car. All big hair and lipstick. But I didn't last long with Sarah – she was the typical high school princess with a new best friend every week. . . . I didn't know Julia well but, for Luke's sake, I hope she's a whole lot sweeter than Sarah.'

'You really liked him, didn't you?' Nanou regarded her granddaughter whose skin was really glowing for the first time in years, her eyes sparkling with a new confidence and awareness of herself as a woman.

'Yes. Yes, I did. But let's not forget he's interested only in how useful I can be.'

'So make yourself useful first and indispensable later.'

'Stop it, Nanou. You just told me he has a fiancée.'

'So he has. But he never mentioned it to *you*.' The old lady almost sniggered.

Luke stared in astonishment as Julia's normally pale face grew crimson with temper as she paced up and down the boardwalk outside her tiny but expensive Docklands apartment. Hands on hips, he stood watching her, making no attempt to pace alongside her. She paused in her march to glare at him.

'Luke, I thought I made it quite clear to you – it's that particular property that I want and no other—'

'And as I've already told you, we can't have it. It isn't for sale.'

'Of course it is,' she snapped. 'Everything's for sale if the offer is generous enough. I've been in love with *Warrender* since the very first time I set eyes on it. Oh – maybe ten or fifteen years ago now. It was so lovely I've never forgotten it. And I made myself a promise that one day it should be mine.'

'Calm down.' Luke was alarmed to see this side of the normally unflappable Julia whose cool blue eyes were usually serene and who could keep her head when everyone around her was in a state of panic. He had always thought of her as the archetypal cool blonde, a woman who would be an asset to both his business and lifestyle. Of course, he wasn't in love with her any more than she was with him; he held no illusions on that score. Some time ago he'd decided that love wasn't something he wanted any more – or the hurt that went with it. His first wife had seen to that – piercing him to the heart with her scorn and bitterness as she blamed him for the death of their son. Julia, he had thought, was cut from a different cloth and it unsettled him to discover she had a vicious temper and was capable of throwing a tantrum like a teenager half her age.

'Julia, be reasonable.' He put a hand on her shoulder only to have it shaken off. 'When I first made enquiries about *Warrender*, I thought it belonged to the old lady who was the last of her line – but that isn't the case. She has a granddaughter and a great grandson as well who expect to inherit.'

'Well, why should they? That place is my Eden. My Shangri-la. No one could love it half as much as I do.'

'But you saw it only once and that was ages ago. You've romanticized it over the years and I'm sure it isn't the place you remember.'

'When I get it, I'll change it all back to the way it was. Luke, I just need your support. I want you to pay those women enough to make them happy to move on and go somewhere else.'

'It isn't as simple as that, Julia. They love *Warrender*, too – it's their family home. Never mind that the garden's a mess and the house needs pots of money spending on it. It's very run down.'

'Neglected, then? So they can't care for it so very much, after all.' Her eyes became chips of pale-blue ice, narrowed at him. 'But I see where you're going with this. You've discovered how much money you'll need to spend to make it habitable and you've gone off the idea.' She stabbed an accusing finger at him. 'You didn't even try to persuade them.'

'Julia, I don't know why we're having this discussion. It's pointless. Forget about *Warrender*. It isn't for sale.' He felt sure that eventually she'd see reason. 'We can find something else. A property overlooking the beach, perhaps.'

She gave a small shiver of distaste. 'No way. I hate the beach. Freezing in winter when the wind blows off the sea and in summer people will park all around us, staring in and leaving their towels and clothing on our back wall.'

'I take your point, but that's not the only solution. If I'm leasing the paddocks and stables next door, we'll have enough room to extend the ranch house at Sunny Orchards – to your very own specifications. How about that?'

'I don't want to build.' She nodded towards her apartment, 'I had enough troubles here getting the tradesmen to come back and make good the cracks when it settled. It will take at least another twelve months to build a decent new house. That shanty you're living in now is barely good enough for your stable manager. No. I've set my heart on *Warrender*. I want to own a piece of Australian pioneer history.'

'But it isn't *your* history, is it? And, in any case, it isn't for sale.'

'We'll see about that,' she muttered.

'Julia, forget about *Warrender*, it's out of reach.'

'It wouldn't be if they still had their backs to the wall. By leasing their stables and employing that wretched girl, you've given them the very means to hold out on us.'

Luke's eyes widened but he made no response. He couldn't tell Julia that he was suddenly very pleased that he had.

Days of furious spring-cleaning in the stables preceded the arrival at *Warrender* of some of Luke's horses. Although both Nanou and Paige rolled up their sleeves and pitched in, it didn't suppress the grumbles of Ham Peachey, the elderly man from the West of England who was their one remaining assistant in the work of the stables. He had a strange accent, a mixture of acquired Australian expressions and his native Devon.

'Dunno why you want to take them extra horses at our time of life, missus,' he said in the midst of sneezing over a bundle of crumbling straw and dust that he was clearing from one of the disused stables. 'An' what of Pierette? She'm not goin' to take kindly to a whole bunch o' new horses.'

'Pierette will be just fine, Ham.' Paige paused in her sweeping to roll her eyes at Nanou who shrugged, indicating that she didn't want to buy into the argument. 'Do her good to have company for a change. And Mr Sandford has no stallions so we won't need to make special arrangements for them.'

'I should hope not. I don't want to be responsible for the likes of them.' Ham was far from reassured. 'I should be windin' down the activity at my time of life, not takin' on more.'

'Ham, you won't have to.' Paige spoke with exaggerated patience, trying not to show her exasperation. 'You will have help here. Mr Sandford is sending two of his own boys to look after them.'

'What? To live 'ere? Does that mean I'll have to share? Boys disturbin' me with the telly an' comin' in all hours of the night?'

Paige smiled, thinking the boys were more likely to be disturbed by Ham's rather musical snoring, but she didn't say so. 'We haven't worked out the details yet. But I think they'll go back to their quarters at Sunny Orchards overnight.'

'Oh, great. Leavin' me to cope with any emergencies after hours.'

Paige sighed. Ham had always been difficult right from day one. She remembered his arrival some twelve years ago when she was still a teenager.

'He may be Peachey by name but he certainly isn't peachy by nature.' She wrinkled her nose, hoping to persuade Nanou to look further and not take him on.

'Unfortunately, no one else seems to want the job.' Nanou smiled ruefully. 'The younger applicants decided they didn't want it when they found out we're not that close to the sea. And an older man will be steadier, more reliable. Peachey comes well recommended and knows his way around horses.'

So Peachey had taken over the well-appointed quarters over the stables and there he had remained ever since. He had no wife, no family and very few friends. Paige had hoped to discover that his gruff exterior concealed a heart of gold but it didn't. Skinny, bald, except for a halo of white fluff around a monk's tonsure and bandy-legged as were most old-fashioned horsemen, Ham was a mean-spirited pessimist who saw only the worst in everyone. And, naturally, as he grew older, his attitude didn't improve. His only redeeming feature was that he did know his way around horses and was devoted to the animals in his charge.

A few days later when the float arrived with the first of Luke's horses, he came to meet it, ready to show those two stable lads who was the boss.

His first setback was to discover that the two 'lads' weren't lads at all, but twin girls, Gail and Glenda Simmons. They had identical pixie haircuts of blonde hair standing in tufts on their heads, identical pointed chins and slanted, almond-shaped green eyes. Ham was suspicious, disliking them both on sight.

'What can they Cornish piskies possibly know about horses?' he muttered, grumbling to himself.

He soon discovered that they knew plenty. They tidied and took over his office that obviously wasn't in use and installed a computer. A closed circuit security system wasn't far behind. And, as well as showing an aptitude for understanding modern technology, they were both expert strappers and stable hands, too. So, try as he might, Ham could find no fault with them, although they teased him mercilessly when he couldn't tell them apart.

Marc adored the two girls and spent as much time as he could in the stables 'helping' them work.

Paige did most of the track work and trials for Luke's horses as well as Pierette and it seemed as if the sharing arrangement was working out well for both of them – until Julia Canning turned up around eight on a Friday evening, shortly after Paige had put Marc to bed. Having made coffee, she was just sitting down in the snuggery to watch television with Nanou when the doorbell rang.

'Who can that be at this time of night?' Nanou frowned. 'Hope it's not Ham to say something's wrong at the stables.'

'Ham wouldn't ring the doorbell. He'd barge right in through the back door,' Paige observed. 'I'll see who it is.'

On the doorstep stood a woman in a black business suit and holding a clipboard as well as a large, black clutch purse.

'I'm sorry,' Paige said, 'whatever you're selling, you'll be wasting your time. We have everything we need.'

'Lucky you, then.' The woman raised one eyebrow and thrust out a hand, introducing herself. 'Julia Canning. I believe you went to school with my little sister?'

'Yes, I did. But—'

'And I'm here to see Mrs Warrender. Can I come in?'

Without waiting for Paige to invite her, she edged past and walked into the kitchen. 'Oh yes,' she said, gazing around at Nanou's herbs and shining copper pots. 'It's exactly as I remember it – I could be in Provence.'

'Why are you here, Miss Canning?' Paige knew she sounded abrupt but she didn't care. 'It's very late to call on anyone without an appointment. We get up early for the horses here.'

'I assure you, it won't take but a moment. As I understand it, your grandmother is the sole owner of the house?'

'Yes, but—'

'Then it is your grandmother that I need to see.'

Hearing voices in the kitchen and the sharpness of Paige's tone, Mrs Warrender came to see what was happening.

'Mrs Warrender! How nice to see you again. You look just the same,' Julia gushed, coming forward to clasp one of the old lady's hands in both of her own. 'I know it's late and I came unannounced, but I really must speak to you. Can we sit down.' She parked herself on a seat at the kitchen table, pulling Mrs Warrender to sit down beside her. Refusing to sit down herself, Paige watched with folded arms. 'Now, then.' Julia's smile was patronizing. 'I do believe you told my fiancé that *Warrender* isn't for sale?'

'Indeed, it isn't.' The old lady drew herself up, looking down her nose at Julia. 'And if that's why you're here, you're wasting your time.'

'Surely not?' Julia gave a tinkling laugh which was entirely false. 'Not if I'm willing to pay you more than a hundred thousand over the estimated price?'

'And why should you do that?' Paige almost snorted with disbelief. 'We don't have pirate treasure buried in the back paddocks, if that's what you think.'

'The house itself is a treasure,' Julia enthused. 'A pioneer homestead, untouched and in original condition.'

'Exactly,' Nanou said crisply. 'That's why it isn't for sale. At any price,' she added quickly before Julia could offer any further argument.

Julia hung her head and sighed. 'Oh, dear. And I felt so sure I could make you an offer you couldn't refuse.'

'Well, I'm sorry but you've had a wasted journey.' It was Paige who spoke. 'You heard what my grandmother said: the house is not for sale.' She glanced at her watch. 'And I'm afraid I can't offer you any refreshment, it's getting late.'

'Paige!' Nanou rebuked her granddaughter, looking a little shocked. It was always her practice to offer tea or coffee to anyone, welcome or not.

'It's all right, Mrs Warrender, I understand.' Julia gave a martyred sigh. 'But I wonder if I could visit your bathroom before I leave.'

'Help yourself.' Paige pointed to the downstairs toilet

just off the kitchen.

'Oh, no,' Julia said. 'I can't use the toilet you offer to tradesmen.' And, before their astonished gaze, she ran for the stairs.

Fifteen minutes later when she hadn't returned, Paige went to look for her, surprised to find her small son standing out on the landing, rubbing his eyes. He reached out towards her and Paige lifted him into her arms.

'What's wrong, sweetheart?' she said. 'Can't you sleep?'

'I was asleep,' he whispered, still on the edge of slumber. 'Mummy, why did that lady come into my room? She didn't say anything and she scared me.' Paige had trouble controlling her fury as she flung open the door of the nursery to find Julia had pulled back the curtain and was gazing out into the gathering darkness, oblivious to the consternation she had caused.

'Miss Canning!' Paige shouted, knowing her raised voice would bring Nanou out into the hall to see what was wrong. 'What are you doing in my son's room?'

'Oh?' Julia sounded bemused. 'Was somebody there? I didn't know.'

'My son, Marc. And you've woken him up.'

'Oh, dear.' Julia ruffled his hair, making the child shy away, hiding his face in his mother's neck. 'So sorry, diddums, I didn't see you.'

'For the second time tonight, I must ask you to leave.' Paige was so angry she could scarcely get the words out. Only the fact that she was holding her son prevented her from shaking the woman until her teeth rattled. She stood, waiting for Julia to descend the stairs ahead of her. Still with Marc in her arms, she opened the front door.

'Go now. And please don't come back.'

'Oh, I'll be back.' Julia twisted her lips into a smile that didn't quite reach her eyes. 'I don't give up this easily.'

When Marc had finally gone back to bed and to sleep, Paige switched off the television, poured a large Bushmills for both Nanou and herself and settled at the kitchen table to talk.

'I'm sure Luke didn't send her.' Nanou opened the discussion. 'It's not his style. Anything he's got to say, he'll say for himself.'

'That's what I thought,' Paige said, sipping her whiskey. 'But I don't think even Luke realizes how determined she is.'

'Don't look so serious,' Nanou laughed. 'We're not selling and the deeds to the house are quite safe in the strong room at the bank. What can she possibly do?'

'I don't know.' Paige gave a small shiver. 'But she'll do something, I know. Marc said he thought she was the bad fairy come to curse him.'

CHAPTER THREE

Luke was delighted with the way Paige was handling his horses. What had commenced as just a convenient arrangement for both of them was proving to be a firm alliance. Scarcely realizing he was neglecting his other business interests as well as Julia, he spent extended weekends at Sunny Orchards, playing a 'hands on' role in training his horses, watching Paige and his other apprentice ride. He even gave her some pointers for improving the performance of Pierette.

'She's a lovely animal,' he said, patting her neck as Paige dismounted to walk the big mare after working her hard. Without even stretching herself, she had beaten one of Luke's best on the training track.

'And definitely not for sale,' Paige rather ungraciously reminded him.

'I'm just admiring.' He continued to pet the animal who nuzzled him in return, hoping for a treat. 'A cat can look at a king.'

'Or a queen.'

'She's got it all.' He was suddenly wistful. 'Strength, stamina and a determination to win. Better than anything I've got at present. With the right preparation she could be a contender for the Caulfield Cup at least, if not the big one in November. If you'll let me, I'd like to help.'

'Hmm. With no strings attached?' she felt bound to ask.

'Sure. I'd do it for the hell of it. It would give me a thrill to see you and your grandmother bring home a Melbourne Cup. A mare owned and trained by women; it would be like Ethereal all over again.'

'You're dreaming,' Paige said and laughed.

'I know. But the dream has to come first before you can achieve anything.'

'Is that how you got to be so successful?' she teased.

Before he could answer, his mobile rang. 'Yes, Lisa?' he said, moving a few paces away to keep the call private as he found out what his assistant wanted. 'Yes, I know I have to choose one of the applicants because you're leaving next week. And I do realize that it's urgent. But look, you know what's needed better than I do. Can't you—?' He listened for a moment and then sighed heavily. 'All right. Appoint the best of them for late morning tomorrow. And no, I can't make it today. And yes, I realize I've been neglecting every-thing for the horses. Just deal with it, Lisa.' He snapped the phone shut without waiting for her reply.

'She's leaving and I have to get a new PA,' he explained, wrinkling his nose. 'I hate change.'

'Most people do,' Paige murmured as his mobile rang again.

'What now?' he growled and blew out his cheeks when he saw it was Julia Canning. 'Yes, Julia? Look I'm in the midst of things right now. Can I call you back? Yes, I know that's what I said yesterday but I—'

Paige wasn't listening to their conversation but she couldn't help overhearing the crisp, staccato tone of Julia's voice, particularly as Luke winced and held the phone

49

away from his ear. She hadn't told Luke about Julia's evening visit to their home, or how furious she had been about the woman's snooping upstairs. He finished the phone call, rather abruptly Paige thought, and she saw that his earlier, happy mood had evaporated.

'I have to go back to town,' he said, looking far from pleased. 'Julia's got some damned social event that we have to go to this evening – a boring dinner for some literary genius and tomorrow it's going to be "pick a PA".'

'Cheer up,' Paige said. 'You could enjoy the party tonight and the PAs might all look like Scarlett Johansson.'

'I wish! Not if Lisa has anything to do with it. She's very careful of my virtue – strictly no distractions in the place of business.' He grinned, some of his good humour restored. 'I'll be back before next weekend, anyway. Meanwhile, you'll have to do the best you can without me.'

'Oh, dear.' Paige pressed the back of her hand to her forehead, mocking him in return. 'How can I possibly survive?'

As it happened, she didn't have to wait that long to see him again. Two of Luke's horses were booked to race mid-week at Caulfield and Pierette was due to run in a mare's race on the same day. Not a major race day but it was still city racing and the competition would be stiff. Paige and Gail Simmons rode in the float with Will, one of Luke's other hands who was driving them to the course. The twins had tossed a coin to see who was to be left behind with the disagreeable Peachey. Glenda lost.

'You owe me, Gail,' she said, after helping them wrap the horses' legs for the journey and adjusting their rugs before loading them into the float.'

Although Paige herself was to ride Pierette, Luke had booked his regular jockey, Taffy Evans, to ride his other two

50

horses that day. As one of the older generation of horsemen, Taffy was reliable, if a little staid. He readily admitted that he had more respect for his bones than to take too many risks. On the plus side, his caution paid off and he could still bring in his share of winners.

Busy as she was with Pierette, whose race was only the second on the card, Paige saw Luke only briefly in the distance, Julia Canning hanging possessively on his arm. He grinned and waved at Paige who was already down in the mounting yard, wearing the Warrenders' distinctive pink and white colours and he gave her a 'thumbs up' for good luck. Seeing this, Julia whipped round to see who he was greeting with such enthusiasm. Her face took on a sullen aspect when she saw it was only Paige.

'Stuck up bitch,' muttered Gail, who had seen the exchange as she steadied Pierette and gave Paige a leg up into the saddle. 'The sooner Luke wakes up to that one the better.'

'Not our business, Gail,' Paige said crisply, at the same time feeling a hypocrite as, secretly, she applauded the comment.

Gail changed the subject at once, talking about Pierette instead. 'This one is a star. Settled beautifully and doesn't mind the crowd. Just interested in everything. I'll be surprised if she doesn't win.'

'Ssh,' Paige said. 'You'll jinx us. The devil has long ears.'

'There's only one devil around here and she's dressed from David Jones rather than Prada,' Gail said as a parting shot as she gave Pierette an encouraging slap on the rump to send her bounding from the mounting yard on to the course.

It wasn't a long race with a field of only ten horses, which was a good thing as the course was relatively small. Paige, aware that the mare was well favoured and therefore a target for other horsemen to hinder, avoided the crush and stayed out of trouble at the rear of the field until she was ready to take control of the race. Gail's assessment was quite accurate. Pierette had not lathered up although for autumn the day was still hot. She was focused and kept in touch with the other horses while showing no tendency to over-race. Paige let her run her own race and didn't ask for speed until the field began to spread out, approaching the home turn. From the position she had held throughout the race, the other riders expected her to move forward around the outside of the field on the grandstand side. As the widest runner, she would have to work doubly hard to over-take them. Instead, although it meant losing a few precious seconds, Paige surprised them by going the other way and seizing the opportunity to slip into the gap they had left on the fence. Pierette, who always responded intelligently, picked up speed, leaving two clear lengths between herself and the rest of the field. Responding to the roar of the crowd, Paige waved her whip as she passed the winning post, exulting in her moment of triumph. It wasn't a major race but it was a nice win and as soon as she had dismounted, returned Pierette to Gail's care and weighed in, she made a quick phone call to share the pleasure of victory with her grandmother. She knew the old lady would have been watching it all on TV.

After changing back into her normal work clothes, she went to help Gail with Luke's skittish gelding, Robin's Lad, due to compete in the next race. He hated crowds and to keep him calm and focused, the two girls walked him between them. Luke came down from the stands to join them and give last-minute instructions to his rider. Paige was surprised to see Taffy eyeing the horse with something like apprehension. Sensing the jockey's anxiety, Robin's Lad acted up accordingly, kicking his back feet and snorting. Paige had heard that older jockeys could sometimes lose their nerve although she had never actually seen it. But Taffy was sweating and wiping his hands down his trousers.

'Hot day,' he muttered giving a half smile, aware of her scrutiny. After playing up and refusing at first to go into his place at the starting gate, Robin's Lad didn't race well and, much as they all expected, Taffy brought him back without gaining a place.

'I'm sorry, mate.' Taffy looked sheepish as he dismounted, giving the horse back to Gail. 'Not feelin' the best. Think I've got the flu or something. Shouldn't ride any more today.'

'But what about Texas Joe?' Luke couldn't hide his exasperation. 'You're down to ride him in the next race?'

'Why not let her take him?' The older man nodded towards Paige, mopping his sweating brow on his sleeve. 'Did a good enough job with that mare.'

'Paige?' Luke raised an eyebrow, hoping she would say yes.

'No, Luke, wait a moment.' It was Julia who spoke, having come down from the stands expecting to lead in a winner. 'You told me this race is important for Texas Joe.' She looked down her nose at Paige. 'Perhaps you should see if there's a more senior jockey available first.'

'Thank you, Julia.' Luke was clearly annoyed by this interruption. 'I don't pass judgement on your business decisions and I certainly don't expect you to criticize mine.'

Julia blinked, shocked to be reprimanded in front of Taffy Evans and the two girls. She said nothing but two bright spots of colour inflamed her cheeks.

53

'Paige?' Luke asked again. 'Are you willing to take the ride?'

'Of course. Texas Joe and I are old friends,' Paige said, but, aware of Julia's simmering resentment, she made sure her smile didn't develop into a smirk. 'If you'll help Gail with Robin's Lad while I go and change.'

'Absolutely,' Luke said, starting to lean in to the horse.

'Luke, your suit!' Julia protested. 'Don't forget we have that reception tonight with cocktails at six.'

'Tonight, is it? Sorry. No can do.' Involved as he was, Luke didn't even look up at her. 'Not that early. Got to make sure the horses are set for home first.'

'Oh, you and your wretched horses.' Having been slighted twice, Julia was in no mood to curb her temper. 'You think more of them than of anyone. Even me!' And she turned on her heel and stamped off, ruining the effect by almost stumbling on her high heels.

Paige ran to change into Luke's colours which Taffy had returned, slightly redolent of stale sweat. Moments later she was back but only just in time to mount Texas Joe before the runners streamed out on to the course.

This was a longer race, requiring different tactics. Texas Joe was an honest horse but he had neither Pierette's instinctive reactions nor a consuming desire to win. He would have to be shown a riding pattern and allowed to stick to it. No last minute changes of direction for him. Paige let him stay on the pace just behind the leaders but she kept him from taking over the lead. She held their position as they reached the home turn, not asking him for a final burst of speed until the leading horses began to tire and drop back, allowing others to take their place. Texas Joe surprised even himself by responding to Paige's hands and heels urging, overtaking the field to win by a short head. Past the post, Paige stood up in the stirrups, whooping and waving her whip although she didn't get the same roar of approval from the crowd as she had received with Pierette. Texas Joe was a long shot and not expected to win. . . .

Up in the stands, Luke was punching the air and celebrating beside a disgruntled Julia who was glancing at her watch and folding her arms.

'Did you see that?' Luke yelled, ready to forget their recent disagreements. 'Paige is a genius. She made that old plodder win!'

'Stop it. You're deafening me,' Julia said. 'I saw what happened. I've got eyes in my head.'

Suddenly, there was a gasp from the crowd and Luke returned his gaze to the course to see Texas Joe running off riderless, pursued by the clerks of the course, and Paige lying in a heap on the turf.

'What happened?' he said. 'I must go down there. She could be hurt.'

'And what can you do, if she is?' Julia protested. 'Let the paramedics, the trained people, deal with it.'

But Luke wasn't listening. He had a horrible sense of *déjà vu*. Of something that had happened five years ago. Black Centurion running away and Ruary McHugh lying fatally injured on the turf. He ran down the steps two at a time and out on to the course.

By the time he reached her, the paramedics had also arrived and, although Paige was obviously shaken, she was slowly getting to her feet.

'What a clumsy idiot.' She smiled ruefully. 'I never fall off.'

'Well, you did today.' Luke peered at her. 'I should've warned you about Joe. It's an old trick of his. Are you sure you're all right.'

'Yes,' she said, taking a deep breath. 'Just a bruise or two, that's all. And now I have to weigh in. Don't touch me anyone, or I could be disqualified.'

'All the same, you should let us check you, miss,' said one of the paramedics. 'You could've broken something.'

'Later,' she said.

But within minutes, she had weighed in and was confirmed as the winner of the race. She came back to Luke smiling although she was still walking gingerly. Julia was still nowhere in sight.

'And you needn't think you're rattling back to *Warrender* with the horses in the float. You put yourself out for me today and now I'll do the same for you. I'm taking you home in the car.'

'Yeah, but what about Julia? And the reception at six?'

'Hang the reception – she can make my excuses,' he snapped. 'I never wanted to go anyway.'

'But—' Paige started to protest. Julia already disliked her. She didn't want her to become a bigger enemy than she already was.

'I'll make it up to Julia, if I have to.' He gave a resigned smile. 'It's amazing what a big bunch of flowers and a trinket can do.'

Paige looked at him for a long moment, realizing for the first time that although he was promised to Julia, he wasn't in love. How would she herself react if she were in Julia's shoes? Would flowers and meaningless trinkets salve her wounds? She didn't think so. She wasn't to be so easily bought.

Julia must have gone off in a huff. To Paige's relief, there was still no sign of her when Luke brought the car round and opened the door for her to get in. She tried not to let him see how much it hurt as she settled herself in the front passenger seat. She had no broken bones but was badly bruised. Luke didn't miss her wince of discomfort.

'Are you sure we shouldn't drop by the hospital and have them check you out?' he said.

'Lord, no. If I went to the hospital every time I got a bruise, I'd be spending my whole life in waiting rooms.'

'I thought you said you never fall off?'

'Do you have to take me up on every word?' She gave him a mock frown. 'The paramedics gave me some Panadol and I'm OK.'

'If you say so.'

They rode in companionable silence on the way home, listening to some of Luke's favourite CDs on a car stereo so good, it felt as if the musicians were actually on stage in front of them. He played *The Blues Brothers* music – so corny it made her laugh – followed by *Eric Clapton Unplugged* and then the music from Baz Luhrmann's *Romeo and Juliet*.

'Oh, I just loved that film.' Paige said. 'Especially the party scene with Mercutio in high heels and drag. Of course we all know the story and how it ends but it still had me on the edge of the seat the whole time. Do you like Shakespeare, Luke?'

'Of course. I'm English, remember? Raised not a stone's throw from the old stamping ground of the bard himself.'

'I've never been to England. I always meant to go but then I got married and never got round to it.'

'Maybe I'll take you one day. Give you the grand tour seen through the eyes of a local.'

Paige glanced at him sharply. It was a flip remark and she knew she wasn't expected to take it seriously. An image of Julia rose in her imagination like an angry genie emerging from a lamp and she shivered.

'Are you cold?' He slowed down to peer at her. 'There's a rug in the back if you need it. You could be in shock.'

'Luke, I'm fine.' She laid a hand on his arm, reassuring him. 'You're making more fuss of me than Nanou.'

'Will you let me buy you dinner on the way home?'

'No,' she said, without hesitation. 'I promised Marc I'd be home to have supper with him and put him to bed. But you can buy fish and chips for us all, if you like, including Nanou.'

'You're on,' he said. 'I love fish and chips out of paper but I haven't had them for years. We'll have calamari and onion rings, too.'

They arrived at *Warrender* with an enormous parcel of seafood which Paige plonked on to the middle of the kitchen table and went to find plates and cutlery. Nanou found tomato sauce and her own special mayonnaise in the fridge.

'Goody, goody!' Marc sang, clapping his hands. 'Fish and chips!'

To make the occasion even more festive, Luke had insisted on buying two bottles of vintage Moët. Nanou blushed like a girl and her fine hazel eyes sparkled when she saw them.

'But surely we should 'ave beer with fish and chips?' she teased.

'Your granddaughter made a lot of money for me today,' he said by way of explanation. 'She rode Texas Joe and got him to win.'

'Really?' Nanou seemed puzzled for a moment. 'But I thought she said Taffy Evans was riding for you today?'

'Not any more,' he said. 'From now on, Paige is my first choice as a rider. Provided that's what she wants?' He smiled at her, raising an eyebrow.

Paige gave a little huff of pleasure and nodded, thinking how their fortunes had turned around. Just over a month ago, Nanou was in tears and she was at her wits' end, wondering how to hold on to *Warrender* and now Luke was offering them money for all kinds of work. All the same, she wasn't completely happy, not with the spectre of Julia looming over them like a bad fairy at a christening.

They entertained Nanou by recounting the events of the day and Marc pretended to enjoy one of Luke's calamari rings. He had been chattering animatedly but now he was stifling huge yawns, ready for sleep.

'Come on, young man.' Paige held out her hand. 'A quick bath for you and then bed.'

'Only if Luke will come up and read me a story,' the little boy said. It was a novelty for him to have a man in the house.

'Mr Sandford to you,' Paige corrected. 'And I don't know if he'll have time. He might want to leave—' She raised querying eyebrows at Luke.

'No. I'll be happy to read you a bedtime story.' Luke promised. ' 'Long as it isn't a whole book.'

'Easy to see you know your way around small boys.' Paige grinned, hoisting Marc into her arms. 'See you in a bit.'

While Luke was upstairs reading the story, Paige and her grandmother washed the dishes and primed the coffee maker.

'That's a lovely man,' Nanou started to say, interrupting herself with a ladylike burp.

'Who is engaged to somebody else,' Paige reminded her.

'Oh, phooey. He'll come to his senses eventually.'

'Interesting. That's what Gail said.'

'Smart girl that one.' The old lady gave another gentle burp.

'I do believe you're squiffy?' Paige laughed. 'How much champagne did you drink?'

'Not my fault. Luke kept filling my glass.' Nanou lowered her voice although Luke was still upstairs reading to Marc. 'And, talking of her ladyship, what became of her? Wasn't she at the races today?'

'She was indeed. And not at all happy about Luke driving me home.'

'I'm sure,' the old lady said with relish. 'She knows competition when she sees it; you have far more in common with him than she does.'

'Well, don't build on it. We have a good business relationship, that's all, I've no intention of ruining that with a dodgy romance.'

Nanou pulled a little face. 'Why do you always 'ave to be so sensible?'

Just then Luke returned, reporting that Marc had fallen asleep. 'I can smell coffee. Great,' he said, watching Paige pour it for all of them offering milk or cream. 'Then I must go. Will I see you in the morning with the horses?'

'I thought you'd be going back to town?'

'You're kidding? Not after all that champagne. And, since I'm here, I'd like you to have a look at Texas Joe again and give me your advice for his next preparation.'

He drank his coffee quickly and headed for the back door. Paige followed, shutting it firmly behind her so as not to be overheard.

'Thank you for today,' she said softly. 'And thanks for being so kind to Marc.'

'Who wouldn't be?' He looked vaguely wistful. 'Lovely chap. He reminds me so much of my own boy at that age.'

60

And, before Paige realized what he intended, he turned and trapped her against the wall by the back door, his hands over her shoulders. Expertly and efficiently, he kissed her surprised open mouth, stirring feelings that had lain dormant for over five years. But before she had time to push him away or respond, he was letting her go again.

'G'night, Paige,' he said with a lazy smile that set her heart thumping. 'That was a good kiss – as good as I always thought it would be.'

'Oh but – you're being so unfair!' she managed to gasp, too breathless and shaken by her emotions to say anything more.

'Yes, I know,' he said. 'I'm a beast. And you probably think I should say I'm sorry but I'm not. I've been wanting to do that all day.'

CHAPTER FOUR

The next day Paige rose early, having slept only fitfully. No matter how many times she told herself it meant nothing, she couldn't let go of the taste and feel of Luke's kiss. She was annoyed with herself for making so much of it. That's what men did – they kissed girls on impulse all the time. It was no more than high spirits – a happy ending to a successful day. And if she allowed herself to make any more of it, then she was a prize fool.

All the same, she kept reliving those moments – the warm smell of his closeness, slightly sweaty at the end of an energetic day, the touch of his warm lips and the gentle intrusion of his tongue. She shivered in delight at the memory, punching her pillow and turning over yet again as sleep continued to evade her.

By the time she arose, shortly before four, she had decided that when she saw him again, she should play it cool. It would be best for both of them if she were to behave as if nothing had happened at all. Because really, very little had. It was only because she had been living a life of celibacy for so long that she was building too much into it. She was as silly as a virgin after receiving her first grown-up kiss. It would mean nothing to Luke who had most likely forgotten about it already.

She dressed quickly in her work clothes and zipped herself into a sleeveless quilted jacket so that she could be warm and mobile. Before going downstairs, she listened outside her door, the rhythmic breathing telling her that Nanou and Marc were still fast asleep. Still a little sore from her fall, she moved about the kitchen, making toast and tea quietly so as not to disturb them. All too aware of Nanou's acute romantic radar, she wanted to get away before she could be captured and quizzed.

At the stables, Ham Peachey was also up early which was unusual. He had already saddled up Texas Joe for her, too.

'That's good of you, Ham,' she started to thank him.

'You have young Robbie to thank for that, not me.' He scowled in the direction of the unfortunate boy who, as the latest arrival, was given the most menial tasks. 'Just hope he did it right.'

'He will have.' Paige smiled at Robbie who saluted her in return. 'But I don't feel like riding today – I'm still a bit stiff. I'll walk him over to Sunny Orchards and let Gail or Glenda take him round.'

Not much interested, Ham shrugged and turned away, his attention taken by another horse. 'Never a moment to meself around here,' she heard him grumble. 'Not these days.'

It was still dark when she reached Sunny Orchards, but unlike the lazy somnolence she had left behind at *Warrender*, the place was already a hive of activity. Gail and Glenda were both out exercising horses on Luke's private track and another boy was supervizing a horse on a walking machine. She glanced around, looking for Luke and steeling herself to greet him casually, but he was nowhere to be seen. And, as soon as Tom Richards, the stable foreman, caught sight of her, he waved a greeting and came over.

'Luke sends his apologies but he had to go back to town. Some emergency at one of the warehouses.'

'Right,' she said, smiling too brightly. No doubt he regretted that kiss already and was now avoiding her, wanting to let things cool for a bit. She would have liked to tell him there was nothing to worry about.

'But he left me with instructions about what he wants you to do – provided you're feeling up to it? He says you had a bit of a mishap after the race yesterday.'

'I'm fine' Paige said automatically, her mind so full of her own thoughts, she was scarcely aware of what Tom was saying. The future was clear to her now. In spite of what anyone said, Luke was marrying Julia, a woman who would be an asset to his business as well as his lifestyle. She, Paige, would never be more to him than a useful employee, a sometime girlfriend, a mistress at best. And she had no intention of letting things slide into that. She couldn't compete with a woman like Julia and she'd end up breaking her heart if she were to try. She could imagine the society columns now – the Sandfords photographed entertaining lavishly from their mansion in Toorak. The golden couple at home in their perfect world. Before long, there might be a baby, too. Another Sandford boy to replace the one lost in Afghanistan. Paige felt an almost physical pain as she tormented herself with these thoughts, but it had to be done. This was the only way to pluck Luke from her heart before he got in too deep.

Dragging her thoughts back to the job in hand as dawn finally broke, she stood beside Tom at the rail, watching one of the twins (Glenda, she thought) putting Texas Joe through his paces. The girl was a good rider and willing to give him his head, letting him dictate his own pace today. But she could see at once that something was wrong. The horse seemed even more skittish than he had been at the races, snorting and breaking pace to skip sideways as if he were trying to dislodge the rider from his back. And then, just as Paige was about to shout a warning, ordering Glenda to dismount, Texas Joe bucked like a rodeo horse, throwing the girl to the ground.

Letting Gail and Tom attend to Glenda who was more surprised than hurt, she set off in pursuit of Texas Joe, hoping he wasn't going to turn into a problem horse. But without a rider he seemed calm and allowed her to catch him easily and walk him back to the stables.

'You're a naughty boy,' she scolded. 'What's got into you, today?'

'It might not be his fault.' Glenda said, when Paige arrived back with him. 'He acted as if there's something under his saddle. I was just about to get off and take a look when he threw me.'

Quickly, Paige unfastened the saddle and discovered a large prickly seed head beneath it, burrowed deep enough to act like a spur. . . .

'Look at that thing!' Glenda said. 'And far too big to have got there by accident.'

'Yes,' Paige said, fingering the burr. 'But then these things can come in with the feed. They're clingy and it was still dark when we saddled up.'

'You did it yourself, then?' Glenda said.

'No,' Paige said slowly, remembering that Robbie had already done it for her. Surely, he wouldn't have done such a thing on purpose, meaning her to be thrown? She shrugged aside the unpleasant thought. 'It's just an accident. Has to be.'

'I suppose,' Glenda said, although she didn't seem entirely happy with this explanation. 'But I'm going to have a word with young Robbie – tell him to be more careful in future.'

After this inauspicious start to the morning, Paige decided to take a break. While the others continued their routine of exercise and Tom ordered a lad to take Texas Joe to a stable, the twins and Paige returned to the office to put the kettle on and make a pot of strong tea. A few moments later, Tom arrived with a big packet of biscuits and soon the incident was forgotten, good humour restored.

That same night, Mrs Warrender was woken by sounds underneath her window, outside the house. She heard trampling and what she thought was boys sniggering, followed by a loud thump and somebody swearing under his breath. She held her breath, straining to hear more.

'Fuck it, Robbie!' someone complained in a harsh whisper. 'Don't care if she is goin' to give us tickets to the concert next week. I hate bloody roses. These thorns are like daggers.'

'Stop trying to climb them, then.' There was an urgent whisper. 'You'll wake the whole household, making that much noise.'

'You'd make a noise, too, if you got ripped apart like me. Look, I'm bleeding. I'll probably die of tetanus.'

'Oh, shut up. We've just got to make it look like attempted burglary. We're not supposed to go in. You were keen enough when I told you about the concert. Why d'you always make such a fuss?'

'I don't like this job. I wish you'd never got me into it. It's too hard.'

'Let's try round the other side of the house, then.'

Able to distinguish little from these mutterings, other than swearing, Mrs Warrender got out of bed and hurried along to Paige's bedroom to wake her.

'Nanou, what is it?' Paige groaned, struggling back from the clutches of the deeper levels of sleep.

'We must call the police,' the old lady whispered. 'I can hear people outside. I think they're burglars, trying to find a way in.'

'Who'd burgle us?' Paige shook her head, still scarcely able to open her eyes. 'There's no money for them in this house. Apart from the horses, we have nothing that anyone could possibly want. It was probably only possums, fighting on the roof.'

'Possums don't argue or say "fuck" when they hurt themselves.'

'All right. All right.' Wearily, Paige threw back the bedclothes and set her feet on the floor. 'Give me a moment to dress and I'll take a look.' She stretched out a hand to put on the bedside light.

'No, don't do that!' Nanou said, in an agonized whisper. 'We don't want them to know we're awake.'

Paige fumbled for her clothes in the dark, shaking her head. She didn't want Nanou to look a fool for calling the police because of the antics of possums.

With her grandmother creeping anxiously behind her, she picked up her grandfather's old cricket bat from a stand on the landing and crept stealthily down the stairs, avoiding the boards that creaked. They stood in the kitchen and listened at the back door, hearing no sound. Cautiously, they peeked around the curtains where there was a view of the whole back yard, directly under Nanou's bedroom window. There was nobody there.

'There you go, Nanou.' Paige said. 'I told you it was just possums.'

'They said they were going to try the other side of the house.'

Of course by the time they went to look there was nobody there.

But in the morning, Nanou was vindicated. They found the footprints of heavy boots outside the kitchen window and bloodstains on the rose that framed it.

Two uniformed police arrived in a patrol car. They examined the bloodstains and the footprints and agreed that intruders must have been there but had been discouraged by the thorns. And, since they had not entered the house and no crime had actually been committed, there wasn't anything to be done.

Mrs Warrender was far from satisfied. 'So,' she said, folding her arms, 'we 'ave to be murdered in our beds and the 'ouse burned to the ground before you can do anything?'

' 'Bout the size of it, ma'am,' the older policeman said. 'But I shouldn't worry too much, if I were you. They won't be back. Most likely kids getting bored and acting up in the school holidays. We get a lot of it at this time of year.'

'And what do you do about it? Nothing!' Nanou was huffing and working herself into a temper. 'Because it makes you no revenue. *Non*. It's easier for you to sit in a speed trap on the main road.'

'No, ma'am. We're not the Highway Patrol,' the younger policeman said, blushing as if he were taking these comments personally. 'And if a crime has been committed, we'll always be here for you.'

'But this is a simple case of trespass, not breaking and

entering,' the older man added.

'They've broken my rose bush,' Nanou said. 'It may never be the same.'

But before her grandmother could take any further issue with them, Paige thanked them for their time and ushered them to the door.

'But I wasn't finished,' Nanou complained when she returned.

'Oh yes, you were,' Paige said firmly. 'You said quite enough. If we keep crying wolf they won't come when we really do need them.'

Luke stayed in town for the rest of the week and Paige heard from Glenda and Gail that he would be travelling to Sydney as he would be taking a couple of horses to the autumn carnival there. Expecting to be asked to ride, Paige wasn't happy about leaving Nanou and Marc in case those youthful intruders returned. But, almost casually, Gail let it drop that Luke preferred to engage local jockeys when he took horses to Sydney.

'The Sydneysiders go round the other way,' Gail said, as if that explained everything. Paige knew this, of course, but it didn't prevent her from thinking that Luke was already regretting his impulse to ask her to ride for him. *Damn the man!* She thought. *Why did he have to kiss me and spoil a perfectly good business relationship?*

So it was a surprise when he called her that evening, friendly and normal as ever.

'I'd very much like to take you to Sydney with me.' He didn't waste his words. 'I'm sending the two fillies up by road with Gail and Glenda to look after them – Happy Rosie who'll be running in the Golden Slipper and also Julia's Gift.'

'And Ms Canning herself – will she be coming to Sydney, too?' The words were out before Paige could think better of them.

'No way.' Luke sighed, sounding irritated. 'She's tied up with some roadies arranging a pop concert on Saturday night – Rod Laver Arena. The latest teenage sensation from England, she says, although I've never heard of them. I'm afraid Julia's Gift is a left-over from our more halcyon days. Julia doesn't show the slightest interest in the animal's progress now.'

'So why are you—?' Paige stopped herself just in time. She'd been about to ask him why he was engaged to a woman he didn't love.

'Why am I what?' There was smothered laughter behind the question.

'Nothing, Luke. It's none of my business.'

'So, if it's all right with you, we'll fly up on Friday. I'd always rather be there the day before. On Saturday we race and come back to Melbourne on Sunday. Gail and Glenda will travel and stay with the horses at the stables of a friend of mine. We offer reciprocal facilities when he comes to Melbourne – not that he often does.'

'Oh Luke, it sounds wonderful and I'd love to – only—' She hesitated, biting her lip.

'Only what? Just tell me what's bothering you, Paige, and I'll fix it.'

'I'm not sure that you can.' Quickly, she told him about their would-be burglars and her qualms about leaving Nanou and Marc alone and unprotected in the house at the weekend.

'Why didn't you tell me about this before?' Luke said. 'I'll get on to it right away. We'll install an alarm system both for your house and the stables and I'll arrange for Robbie

70

to bunk in with Ham.'

'Robbie!' Paige said, thinking of the burr under Texas Joe's saddle. 'Ham doesn't really get on with him. Can't you send Will?'

'Whatever you say. And just for good measure I'll book a security guard to keep watch on the place overnight.'

'Far as I'm concerned, Luke, that sounds great, but I don't think Nanou will like it.'

'Then she'll have to lump it.' He came right back at her. 'I need you to have your mind on the job and can't have you worrying about what's happening down here in Melbourne while we're away. The tickets are already booked; we're flying to Sydney on Friday at two o'clock, avoiding the late afternoon rush.'

'Really?' She felt a small tickle of irritation. 'You must've been very certain I'd go.'

'Not at all.' He sounded amused by her tone. 'But I'd rather cancel a ticket than not have a seat available when I want one.'

Paige was right. Nanou wasn't at all pleased at the thought of having an alarm system installed in her home.

'I'm sure to forget and keep setting it off,' she grumbled.

'All right. If you really don't want it, I'll have to tell Luke I won't go. He's not going to be very pleased about that.'

'Oh no, no. You 'ave to go. But I wish he'd given you a bit more notice. What are you going to wear in the evening? You have nothing new.'

'So what? I'm riding for him, Nanou. We're not going dining and dancing.'

'More's the pity.' The old lady sniffed. 'People used to have a sense of occasion in my day.'

Even so, Paige included her one good little black dress in

her luggage and a pair of high-heeled pumps, although she didn't mention this to Nanou.

'I want to go to Sydney with Luke,' Marc pouted, when she told him where she was going and kissed him before leaving. 'I like him.'

'Just be a good boy for Nanou. It's only for two days – we'll be back before you know it. And I'll call you on Saturday evening after the races. They'll be on television all day – you might even see me.'

She gave him another quick hug and left before he could make any more objections. As she was using public transport and taking the airport bus from the city, she wanted to make sure she was there in plenty of time. All the same, Luke managed to arrive at the airport before her together with Julia, made up to the nines with every blonde hair in place and looking her immaculate best in a new suit the colour of autumn leaves. Paige's heart sank as she murmured a greeting, thinking Julia must be coming to Sydney after all. She looked Paige up and down without greeting her, clearly unimpressed with what she saw.

'I see you're taking your track rider,' she said to Luke. 'Is that really necessary? Or wise? I thought you booked local jockeys in Sydney?'

Luke smiled, refusing to rise to the bait. 'I told you, Paige is my regular rider now, wherever we race.'

Julia shrugged and glanced at her watch. 'I must go. Sorry I can't wait to see you off.'

'That's OK.' Luke gave her a perfunctory kiss on the lips without taking her into his arms. 'Thanks for the lift. Hope the concert goes well.'

'Should do. It's a sell out.' Julia turned away, her mind already on other things. Paige noticed she didn't reciprocate his good wishes or even wave goodbye. It struck her as a cold leave-taking, not at all like that of a couple about to be married; a couple in love.

After Julia left, there were a few moments of awkward silence between them. Paige filled it by checking in her bag at the counter and receiving her boarding pass.

Luke glanced at his watch. 'Still half an hour till we board. Coffee?' he offered.

'No, thanks,' Paige said. 'I have a cup of strong coffee in the morning to get me going but it makes me jumpy if I keep having it throughout the day.'

'I see,' he said, watching her fidget with her pony-tail, glancing around and blinking, not quite at ease. 'And you don't really like flying, do you?' he hazarded a guess.

'Does it show?' She grinned ruefully. 'It's not that I'm scared for myself – after all people fly every day. It's just when I think about Marc.'

'Marc?'

'I think – what will happen to my little boy if I die in a plane crash? He only has Nanou and she's over seventy. There is no one else: Ruary's mother died not long after he did.' She didn't go on to mention that although Lyddie's death was officially accidental, the rest of the family knew it was suicide.

Luke cut across the thought. 'Paige, this is only a local flight. It takes less than an hour. I promise you nothing is going to go wrong.'

'I'm being foolish, I know. But you did ask.'

'Perhaps a brandy, then? To settle your nerves.'

'No, Luke. I don't like to drink alcohol when I'm riding to race the next day.'

He blew out a long breath. 'How very proper. I wish all jockeys were as conscientious as you are.'

'I have to be. I'm a woman trying to compete in a man's

world. So much more is expected of us.'

Luke considered this, looking thoughtful.

They boarded their flight as soon as it was called, travelling economy as they would be in the air for less than an hour. Paige allowed Luke to take the window seat as she didn't like watching the ground drop away when the plane left the runway and took to the skies.

Half an hour into the trip, she began to relax. She'd enjoyed a glass of fresh orange juice and was almost on the borders of sleep when the plane shuddered as if being shaken by a giant hand, the roar of the engines suddenly unusually loud. Her eyes snapped open. What could that be? Turbulence? She glanced up but no warning light had come on telling people to fasten their seat belts and the staff were still going about their business having distributed drinks.

Without any warning at all, the left wing dipped, turning the plane completely on its side. Drinks shot all over the place and the engines screamed as the plane shuddered yet again. Seconds later, it went into a nose dive, dropping like a stone. Paige whimpered and Luke tried to put a protective arm about her as they were both slammed against the back of the seats in front of them. Paige closed her eyes, bracing herself for the inevitable collision with the earth, hoping the end would be quick. She had heard of people in plane crashes being roasted alive. It didn't help to know it was nobody's fault but her own. She had tempted providence by talking about a crash and now Luke and their fellow passengers were about to die along with her. The sensation was like that of being on the worst kind of roller coaster in free fall.

Some people were screaming in terror, raw ape-like sounds that rasped the nerves, while others howled and wept. Surprisingly, some gave way to hysterical laughter. It was a cacophony of human terror, everyone quite certain these were their last moments of life and the plane was doomed.

Moments later, the plane righted itself and the terror was over almost as suddenly as it had begun. The pilot regained control, lifting them to the right altitude once more and the journey continued as if nothing had happened. Stewards raced up and down the aisles, asking the passengers if anyone had been hurt but it seemed, apart from some bruising, nobody had. There were few elderly people aboard so no one had suffered the complication of a heart attack or a stroke.

Paige sat there unable to stop shivering, feeling as if she had wished it upon them and clinging to Luke's hand with both her own. It was a strong, brown hand, surprisingly warm and comforting. He, too, had nothing to say, perhaps feeling guilty for being so certain nothing would go wrong. Ten minutes later the pilot explained that they had been caught in the jet stream of a much larger aircraft, travelling at the same altitude. This had been enough to knock them off course momentarily. He concluded by saying there was no further need for alarm; everything was now normal and under control.

The remaining thirty minutes of the flight seemed to last forever. Everyone seemed fearful and tense, unable to believe it wouldn't happen again. But the journey was over at last without further event, the only difference being that the pilot stood alongside the stewards, watching his passengers file past as they left the aircraft. Perhaps he needed to reassure himself that no one had been seriously hurt. There were no further apologies or explanations and they were never told if the mistake was made by traffic control or if pilot error was to blame. Fortunately, everyone had escaped with no more than a few bruises and frayed nerves.

'You're having that brandy now, whether you like it or not.' Seeing Paige's white face, Luke picked up their luggage from the carousel and headed for the bar. 'You're in shock.' Too shattered to protest, she followed on unsteady legs.

To stop them from trembling, she clutched the brandy balloon in both hands, sipping it as if it were medicine. Luke tossed his down in one go and went back for a refill.

'Are you sure you feel up to riding tomorrow?' he asked her when he returned.

Paige laughed weakly. 'Why not? I've got to get rid of all this adrenaline somehow.'

Another surprise awaited her when she reached their hotel – luxurious, of course, and with picturesque views of the harbour. But, instead of booking her a separate single room as she expected, Luke had taken a suite. She saw at once that it did contain two separate bedrooms, but she hadn't expected them to be sleeping in such close proximity. It occurred to her that Julia wouldn't approve, but quickly banished the thought. Nanou, of course, would expect her to take shameless advantage and the wicked imp on her shoulder advised the same but she crushed the thought before it could take root.

In the early part of the evening, Luke left her in peace to settle in. There was a comfortable queen-sized bed in her room as well as a small TV and also a private bathroom of her own. It was a suite designed to accommodate a family rather than honeymooners.

Meanwhile, Luke sat at the desk in the sitting-room to

catch up on work and make a few phone calls. He told her he wanted to check that the twins and the horses were safely settled in and all ready for their day at the races tomorrow.

Half expecting not to see him again until morning, Paige decided on an early night. The near death experience had shaken her more than she had first realized. But a hot shower calmed her still further. Afterwards, she changed into her rather child-like flannelette pyjamas and lay on the bed reading a murder mystery someone had left in the drawer of the table beside the bed. It was something of a surprise then when Luke knocked at the door shortly after seven o'clock.

'In bed already,' he said, hovering in the doorway. 'I was thinking of dinner. There's a bistro downstairs – but if you'd rather have something sent up?'

'No. I can get dressed again.' Paige sprang off the bed, deciding she'd had more than enough of her own company. 'I can be ready in five.'

She pinned her errant curls into a casual topknot and dressed quickly in her little black dress. Still pale from her ordeal, she added a little rouge to make her eyes sparkle, mascara to lengthen her rather pale lashes and a touch of pink lip gloss.

'Wow,' he said when she emerged from her room. 'You look great.'

'Well, your jockey has to be a credit to you, doesn't she, Mr Sandford?' she grinned.

The hotel offered several kinds of dining – the formal style with the head waiter dressed in tails, and his minions like old-fashioned bell-hops, and there was also a French-style bistro with cosy alcoves and waiters wearing over-sized aprons, grinding pepper over people's meals and dispensing chunks of warm, home-made bread. Luke chose the bistro and they occupied one of the alcoves.

'I'm not sure if I'm hungry or not after all that drama,' she said.

'Now you stop that right now.' He fixed her with a stern look. 'You'll only trap it there forever if you keep replaying it in your head.'

'It's not something I can readily forget. Just shows how easily things can go wrong.'

Luke ignored this, speaking to the wine waiter instead. 'We'll start with a bottle of vintage Moët and—'

'Luke, no! I told you I never drink before a race.'

'Tonight, you do. Even if I have to put away most of it myself. We're not driving and anyway, you're not racing till after three.'

'I know, but—'

'No buts. Not tonight. And what will you have to eat? I thought a dozen oysters for starters.'

She gave him a slow smile that developed into a wicked pixie grin. 'Oysters and champagne? What are you trying to do to me, Mr Sandford?'

'Me?' He opened eyes wide with mock innocence. 'I'm just trying to give a girl a good time.'

The oysters were delicious – *au naturel* – large and succulent with just a squeeze of lemon juice to help them down. The first dozen seemed to disappear so quickly, they asked for more, washing them down with the delicious sparkling wine. After this, they had room only for a slice of quiche and a green leaf salad. Paige had been careful to drink only one glass of champagne and although Luke had finished the bottle it didn't seem to affect him.

'Now for a nightcap.' He signalled the wine waiter to return to their table. 'I'll have a double brandy and a champagne cocktail for the lady.' This time the order was given before Paige could protest. With Luke in this mood, it would be useless to do so, anyway.

CHAPTER FIVE

Paige wasn't aware that Luke was really quite drunk until they got into the lift. He slung an arm around her shoulders and staggered a little as he pressed the button for their floor, smiling at this moment of weakness. On glancing up at him, she saw that his eyes were dreamy with lust, his gaze focusing on her slightly parted lips. His hand was lying possessively on her shoulder, giving her little doubt of his intentions and her heart stepped up its beat. Of course, she should have expected it. Having wined and dined her, he was now ready to take her to bed. The possibility of rejection wouldn't cross his mind. Assured of his own attraction, he would take it as a matter of course. She recalled the old show-business adage – *anything that happens on location stays on location* – it doesn't count. Did he consider that they were on location now – 500 miles away from everyday commitment and responsibility?

And how did she feel about it herself? She was a realist and already knew that she wanted him – she didn't need her French grandmother to tell her that. But was she capable of going through with it and coming out unscathed? Could she indulge herself, take whatever he offered at face value and then walk away? No. She knew herself better than that. She wasn't made that way. If she gave in to her passions and allowed him to pleasure her with no thought to the future, the emotional fall out and cost would be far too great.

So she let his arm stay where it was even as he opened the door to their suite but firmly removed it as soon as they were inside.

'Thank you for a lovely evening, Luke,' she said rather unsteadily, refusing to meet his gaze. 'I had a great time.'

'Oh, Paige—' He could hardly speak, attempting to catch her again and draw her towards him. But his reactions were slowed and she was too fast for him, making it to the door of her room in two quick strides. 'Just stay a moment and talk.'

'Uhuh. Big day tomorrow,' she murmured, still unable to look at him. If she did, she knew for certain that she would be lost. 'Best get some sleep.'

On the other side of the door, unable to trust him not to follow her, she turned the key as quietly as she could and then leaned with her ear pressed against it, hoping to hear what he was doing on the other side. She heard nothing, apart from the fridge door opening and then slamming. He was probably getting himself another drink.

Alone in her bed, much as she expected, sleep evaded her. She punched the pillow and started calling herself all kinds of a fool. She was a disgrace to her French ancestors who had been courtesans since before the French Revolution – or so Nanou said – every one of them beautiful, too. Nor did it help her to realize she had acted from cowardice rather than virtue. If she had followed her inclinations and allowed nature to take its course, she and Luke would have been sleeping soundly by now, satisfied and replete in every sense.

81

Midnight came and went. When the digital clock on the bed-head tripped over to register one a.m. she got up and put the kettle on while she went to have a warm shower. There were packets of herbal tea on offer, as well as the usual instant coffee; a cup of camomile tea might help her to settle for what remained of the night.

She came out of the shower with one fluffy white towel wrapped around her and a smaller one around her head to hear someone tapping softly at her door. It could only be Luke.

'Paige,' he called softly. 'I know you're awake in there, I can hear you. Can we talk?'

It took her only a moment to unlock the door. He stood there dishevelled but still fully dressed although he had taken off his jacket and tie. His trousers were badly creased from where he had been lolling about in them. He must have been scrubbing his fingers through his hair because it was standing on end. There was an uncertain expression in his dark eyes as if he were unsure of his welcome. Paige had never set eyes on a man that she wanted more in the whole of her life.

They gazed at one another for a long moment saying nothing and then she walked straight into his arms, breathing in the musky scent of him as she linked her own arms around his waist. He was a tall man and she was a tiny woman; barefoot she was scarcely as high as his heart.

Their first real kiss was everything she had always thought it would be. It felt so right, so wonderful, it was like coming home. He tasted of good whisky and coffee. As she leaned in to him, the towel fell away from her head. But, aware that she was vulnerably naked under the bath towel, he didn't try to undo it but enveloped her, towel and all, in the warmth of his embrace. She was breathing heavily now, thoroughly aroused by his attentions and she unfastened his shirt and stood on the tips of her toes to leave a trail of kisses along his collar bone, tasting the warm, salty flesh beneath her teeth.

Finally convinced of her willingness, he let the towel fall to the floor and, finding her lips again, kissed her soundly before sweeping her into his arms and carrying her to his bed which she saw had not been slept in as yet. Scarcely able to speak as they were both trembling so much from anticipation and a sexual hunger that caught both of them by surprise, they came together as naturally as if they had been lovers forever. It was more than five years since Paige had made love to anyone. As a widow, sharing a home with her grandmother, she had been living the life of a nun. But somehow, in the midst of their frantic lovemaking and wanting to be so close they were almost one person, she registered that Luke was just as carried away, as out of control and needy as she was. That near death experience on the plane must have brought them to the same pitch of urgency and passion. She cried out, straining towards him as he thrust inside her before claiming her lips yet again. He was considerate, making sure that her cries were of passion rather than pain before they reached a combined orgasm which left them both flushed and breathless as they came back to earth again, staring in wonderment into each other's eyes.

And later, when they had made love a second time in more leisurely fashion, he fell into a sated, contented sleep with one arm flung across her and his warm breath tickling her neck. Paige closed her eyes, on the border of sleep herself and thinking how wonderful, how right it seemed to be sharing his bed.

Suddenly, her eyes snapped open and she was wide

awake as if a bucket of cold water had been thrown over her. Neither one of them had given a moment's consideration to birth control or safe sex. Panic engulfed her as it dawned on her how irresponsible they had been.

Gently, she extricated herself from the bed without waking him and ran to the bathroom. She studied herself in the mirror and frowned at her reflection, shaking her head. She looked as if she had been taking part in a drunken orgy. Her lips were swollen and bruised from the violence of his kisses and there was an angry love bite at the base of her throat. Grimly, she remembered she had left a similar one of her own on him. Let him explain that to Julia! Thinking of Julia made her wince. 'Location' no longer seemed all that far from home.

Watching herself in the mirror, she traced the outline of her nipples rosy and prominent from so much attention after being hidden and ignored for so long. Aware of a tenderness and stickiness between her legs, she made use of the bidet, grateful for the amenities of top class hotels. She could only hope this precaution would not be too late. Surely, she couldn't get pregnant just from one night? But didn't everyone say it was easy for a woman to fall when she had already given birth? She closed her eyes, imagining the worst scenario – two children to raise on her own and curtains for her career as a professional rider. It had been hard enough to exercise back to fitness after giving birth to Marc and she was five years older now; it was unlikely that she could do it all over again. Her usefulness to Luke would be at an end.

She drew a shuddering breath, pulled one of the hotel dressing gowns tightly around her and went back to his room to find him lying in bed awake, supporting himself on one elbow and waiting for her to come back. He smiled, having no inkling that anything might be wrong.

'I missed you,' he said, patting the empty space beside him. His smile faded when he saw her bleak expression. 'Paige, what's wrong? I know I got a bit carried away – we both did – but I didn't hurt you, did I?'

'No, Luke, it's not that. It's just – I didn't think ahead because I wasn't expecting this and – um – we didn't use any birth control—'

'Oh, is that all? You had me worried there for a moment. Oh, I know it looks bad for me – jumping you on our first night – but I really don't make a habit of sleeping around and I'm sure you don't, either.' Surprisingly, he laughed.

'It's not funny, Luke. I've already had one child and if I fall pregnant again, I won't be able to ride, not profession-ally anyway. I need to maintain a certain level of fitness and if I have another baby, I won't get it back.'

'I'm not laughing at you, love.' He was suddenly serious. 'But you can't fall pregnant – not by me, anyway. I've had a vasectomy.'

She stared at him. 'But why? Why would you do that?'

'Because of Rachel, my wife. She had such a bad time having Alan, she swore she'd never go through the pain of childbirth again. She wouldn't resume relations until it was done.'

'But that's so unfair.' Paige felt a rush of compassion as she realized that in losing Alan, Luke had lost so much more than his only child. He had no possibility of being a father again. No wonder he looked at Marc with such wist-fulness, thinking of the children he could no longer have.

'Can it be reversed?'

'I wouldn't know.' He shrugged. 'I've never pursued the idea.'

'But what about Julia? Won't she expect to have children?

Have you told her?' As usual, the words tumbled out before she could stop them.

His expression clouded and he sighed. 'Do we really have to talk about Julia now? This is our time.'

She stared at him, absorbing what he'd just said. If they were to mean anything to each other, they would eventually have to talk about Julia. Unless – and it came to her in a flash – this really wasn't anything more to him than an 'on location' adventure. *This is our time*, he had said. Meaning that when they got back to Melbourne it would be over between them. What a fool she had been to think otherwise; to take him so seriously.

'No, of course not,' she managed to stammer through lips that were suddenly stiff. 'It's really none of my business.' So saying, she hugged the dressing gown more closely about her, suddenly chilled. 'I should go and get some rest in my own bed. I'll be good for nothing in the morning.' And, averting her gaze so that he wouldn't see the gathering tears in her eyes, she ran for the sanctuary of her own room before he could stop her.

'Paige, come back here,' he called after her. 'What is it? What did I say?'

She didn't answer him and this time she didn't muffle the sound of the key turning in the lock. Still in the dressing gown, she threw herself into bed, pulled the bedclothes over her head and buried her face in the pillow to stifle the sound of her weeping. Soon, although it was the last thing she expected, she fell asleep.

She overslept and woke to the sound of Luke hammering on the door. 'Wake up, sleepyhead!' he was saying. 'We've missed breakfast and we ought to be at the track. We can grab a coffee on the way.'

She showered and dressed as fast as she could, wondering if the twins would be able to guess how she'd spent the night. She studied herself in the mirror but, apart from the hollows under her eyes and the bruised tenderness of her lips, she didn't think she looked too bad. Any other evidence was hidden under her clothes.

As Rosehill Gardens was some distance from the city and the journey would take over half an hour, Paige was relieved when Luke sat in front to make conversation with the taxi driver, avoiding the need for small talk between them. He was probably feeling as awkward as she did about the previous night.

As soon as the driver found out they were racing people, he entertained them with tales of other well-known racing personalities who had been in his cab as well as pestering Luke for a list of likely winners. Luke deftly avoided that trap, saying he knew nothing of any runners except his own horses.

On arrival at Rosehill Gardens, mercifully, routine took over. Paige excused herself quickly to establish herself in the girls' changing room. Then she went to the stables to catch up with Glenda and Gail who were already there, taking care of the horses.

'My God, Paige, what happened to you?' Glenda greeted her with no thought of tact. 'You look an absolute fright. Are you sick?'

Paige smiled weakly, realizing she must look worse than she thought. Quickly, she recounted the story of the incident on the plane, hoping the twins would accept that as the reason for her hollow eyed pallor and lack of sleep.

'Ooh, that's horrible,' Gail chimed in. 'Makes me glad to be travelling with the horses. Poor you. Will you have to fly back?'

'I don't know,' Paige said slowly, not having thought about this. She had been so relieved to reach terra firma in Sydney, she had given little thought to the journey home.

Julia's Gift was to run in one of the earlier races before the Golden Slipper. One of the highlights of the Sydney racing calendar, the Slipper was promoted as being the highest paid race for two year olds in the world and a good crowd always turned out to see it.

'Our carnival is a celebration of youth,' one of the speakers proclaimed as he accepted his prize. 'Young horses as well as young people.'

Paige sighed. She wasn't feeling so young herself right now and her body still ached after all that unaccustomed athletic activity last night. No! She mustn't go down that path, she reminded herself. It wouldn't do to let herself dwell on thoughts of Luke or his wonderful body. She must keep her mind on the job.

Although she was well acquainted with Happy Rosie, Julia's Gift wasn't one of the horses she had ridden for Luke before. The filly seemed placid enough – perhaps even too much so – as she ambled around the mounting yard, unaffected either by Paige on her back or the raucous shouts of the crowd before they increased speed and moved out on to the track.

'Haven't seen you in Sydney before.' One of the local jockeys made conversation as they walked the horses around, waiting to go into the starting gates. 'First time, is it?'

Paige nodded and smiled, not wishing to be drawn. She wanted to size up her opposition and focus on the race. It was only 1000 metres so there wouldn't be much time to correct anything if she missed the start.

Julia's Gift was a solid performer and quickly took up a position with the leaders on the fence. For a while there,

Paige believed she was going to hold them all off and win from this leading position but over the last few yards two horses charged past her in unison, robbing her of victory and leaving her to be satisfied with third place.

'I'm so sorry.' She pulled a wry face at Luke as she gave the sweated-up filly back to Gail.

'No, you did well,' he reassured her. 'I only brought her as company for Rosie – didn't really expect her to do anything.'

'Oh.' Paige began to feel better than she had felt all day. 'But you do hope for a better result from Rosie?'

'I always hope. But I don't know who'll win the Slipper – nobody does. It's the richest race and everyone wants the prestige of winning it. These horses are young and mostly untried. But Rosie has a will to win and we've done all we can to prepare her. All I ask is that you go out there and do your best together.'

'We will.' She gave him a genuine smile that was no longer tempered by caution. 'You bet we will.'

'I might do that, too,' he said, glancing at his watch. 'There's just about time.'

Showers earlier had now given way to clear skies as they lined up in the starting gates before the running of the Golden Slipper. Paige looked along the line and saw that as well as people she did not know, she would be competing with several high-profile jockeys from both Sydney and Interstate. One Sydneysider in particular was quite a celebrity; an older jockey, famous for having the knack of winning a feature race. It was said of him that he wouldn't get out of bed to race unless he thought he could win. Paige resolved to travel with him, hoping Rosie would keep up when he let down his mount for the finish.

There was no time to think of anything else because they were off. Paige was badly jostled as they came out of the starting gates but Rosie wasn't upset and quickly recovered her stride. Paige could see the high-profile jockey mid field, keeping his mount clear of the horses beginning to tire and she urged Rosie forward to catch him up. As she drew level, he glared at her, afraid that Rosie was going to crash into him but Paige held her clear, not wanting to be accused of interference. She was still keeping pace with him as they rounded the home turn and he gave his mount a good crack of the whip to get him going.

Just as she hoped, Rosie continued to keep pace with him, although Paige resorted to hands and heels to encourage the filly, rather than use her whip. The two horses thundered towards the winning post with the rest of the field left far behind and for a moment Paige thought she might be just a little too late. But Rosie had the makings of a champion and wouldn't accept defeat. Somehow she produced an extra stride to win the race by just half a head.

The Sydney jockey was gracious in defeat although his smile was a little rueful. 'Well done,' he said, congratulating Paige. 'You rode that race exactly as I should have done in your place.'

'Thanks.' Paige grinned at him, only now allowing herself to think of the prize money and what her portion might be. She couldn't wait to call Nanou and tell her the good news until she remembered that they would have been watching it all on television at home.

As soon as correct weight was called, Luke gave another whoop of delight, grabbed Paige and whirled her around before giving her a smacking kiss on the cheek. Aware of the television cameras trained on them, she tried to signal caution. They had just won a major race. Didn't he realize it would be broadcast across the whole country, if not the rest of the world?

Speeches had to be made which she always hated and finally they were free to go. Along with their driver, Gail and Glenda were already preparing the horses for their journey home and Paige wondered if anyone would think it odd if she asked to go with them. So far as Luke was concerned, she had no intention of making the same mistake twice.

As it happened, there was no time. The twins were anxious to get the float on the road and Gail had a boyfriend who was coming to meet them at Albury on the way home.

'Now then,' Luke said, when they were finally back at the hotel, alone. 'The Slipper aside – which was wonderful, by the way, and largely thanks to you – what happened last night? I could see you were upset? Was it something I said?'

'Nothing really – I was just being silly.' Once again she was finding it difficult to meet his gaze.

'Oh come on, Paige. I deserve better than that. I'm not so crass that I'm insensitive to your moods.'

'Luke, last night was special. Well, it was to me, anyway. But I can't let it happen again. You're still engaged to Julia.'

'Not for long. Julia and I are about to break up.'

'Does she know that?'

'Well, I haven't spelled it out in so many words, but—'

'So it hasn't happened yet. And I don't want to be the catalyst.'

'You won't be.' He sighed. 'It's senseless to go on because it's been dead between us for a long time. I don't know what's got into Julia. When we first met, she seemed to me so calm, so self-possessed – she had all the qualities I admired most in a woman. Lately, she's turned into a nervy harridan.'

And I'd turn into a harridan, too, if I thought I was losing you. Paige thought, reminding herself that Luke Sandford wasn't – or ever likely to be – hers to lose.

'But you must have been in love with her once? At the beginning, at least?'

'Perhaps. I was interested, yes. In love? I'm not so sure. We didn't really know each other – and now that we do, it turns out we're not suited at all. She isn't interested in horses or racing and I can't raise any enthusiasm for pop concerts. I'm sure she'll be reasonable when I point it out. She just needs to see it, that's all.'

Not for the first time, it occurred to Paige that Ms Julia Canning would not let go of her prize so easily.

'Enough solemn faces.' Luke clapped his hands, immediately changing his mood. 'We have a win to celebrate.'

'Oh, Luke, I'm so tired, I don't think I could face dressing up to go out—'

'There's no need. We'll send out for Chinese and have it up here. And, by the way, I don't want you worrying about the return flight because I've cancelled it. I'm hiring a car and we're driving back to Melbourne instead.'

'But won't everyone be expecting you back tomorrow?' she said softly, still thinking of Julia.

'So what?' He shrugged. 'And besides, I have something I want to show you on the way.'

'But Luke,' she said, staring at him, 'you didn't have to hire a car. You could've sent me back with Glenda and Gail in the float.'

'So I could. But being selfish, I wanted you here tonight, celebrating with me.'

Paige's heart lifted. As usual, she couldn't resist him. 'All right, I give in,' she said, taking his hand in agreement. 'But not before I speak to Nanou and Marc.'

She made the call while Luke went to shower and change. Marc must have grabbed the phone before Nanou could reach it, certain it would be his mother.

'Mummee!' he yelled, almost deafening her. 'You won. We saw it all on TV.' His mood changed as the sound of her voice made him realize how much he was missing her. 'But I want to see you. When are you coming home?'

'Soon.'

'I don't like *soon*. It means not tomorrow.'

'We're coming by car so it might take a day or two, yes.'

'But why?' The little boy was becoming querulous. 'I miss you, Mummy, and I need you now.'

'I know, darling, I miss you too, but I'll be home before you know it. I send you a big kiss goodnight, but now let me talk to Nanou.'

She heard the little boy reluctantly giving up the phone.

'Congratulations!' Nanou said. 'I knew you could do it. And how's everything going with Luke? I saw him whirling you around.'

'As did everyone, I'm sure. Don't worry. He was just pleased with the good result.'

'Back home tomorrow, then?' Nanou sounded vaguely disappointed.

'No,' Paige said slowly. 'And you'll gather Marc's not too pleased about it, either. Luke's hired a car and we're driving.'

'Oh, really?' The old lady's voice was eager with innu-endo. 'What brought that on?'

'It's a long story and I don't have time to tell you over the phone.'

'Oh, but I can guess.' Nanou's tone was triumphant. 'The

apple doesn't fall that far from the tree.' She lowered her voice. 'You slept with him, didn't you?'

'Stop it, Nanou, you're embarrassing me.'

'Only because it's true.' The old lady crowed with delight. 'You take just as long as you want, *cherie*. Marc will be fine with me.'

At ten o'clock on that Saturday evening, Luke's night watch security guard made his rounds and once again helped Mrs Warrender to set the alarm.

'What a waste of time and money.' She clicked her tongue at him, irritated by the need to understand its intricacies before locking up the house for the night.

'I'll be checking outside again in an hour or so,' Kevin Mitchell said, ignoring her remark. 'Mr Sandford wanted me to take special care.' An ex-army man, Mitch's security business was his own and he was conscientious, doing the lion's share of the work himself, employing others only when his workload demanded it. This was the first job he'd had from Luke Sandford and he wanted to make a good impression. 'Now you have my mobile number and I want you to call me if you're worried – about the slightest thing.'

'But, Mitch, it all seems so—'

'Unnecessary, Mrs Warrender, I know. But Mr Sandford's orders were very specific. He'd rather see you safe than sorry. The stables, too. Now, you'll make sure you double lock all your doors when I've gone?'

'Yes, yes. I'm beginning to feel that I live in a fortress.'

'G'night, then.'

'Goodnight, and thank you, Mitch.' The old lady smiled at last, always ready to be charmed by a good-looking young man. And Mitch was good-looking in a 'no nonsense – action man' way. 'I'm an old grump, I know.'

*

Around midnight, Marc came into her room to wake her.

'Nanou, I'm frightened,' he said. 'There are lots of big boys in cars outside. They want to know where the party is.'

The old lady stretched and put on her robe before getting out of bed. 'Don't be scared, Marc. They don't mean any harm. They've just made a mistake and come to the wrong address. You stay here in my bed and I'll send them away.'

She put on the light and threw up the sash window to speak to them, astonished to see about ten vehicles outside the house with more cars arriving, blocking the drive behind them. There were a lot of people gathering there.

'About time!' one of the boys yelled when he spotted her. 'We're here for the party. Open up, Gramma!'

'I'm sorry.' Seeing so many people swarming around, Nanou was beginning to feel less than assured and her voice shook when she raised it to speak to them. 'But you've made a mistake. There's no party going on here.'

Several of the boys glanced at each other.

'But hey! This is *Warrender*, isn't it?'

'Yes, it is, but—'

'The bash was advertised on the net. *Come one, come all to Warrender on the Peninsula – Saturday night.* There was even a Melway reference and a map. *Party the night away with free beer and wine.* Come on, ol' lady, don't keep us standing out here. Open up.'

Mrs Warrender closed the window and dialled Kevin Mitchell's number with shaking fingers. It was probably only a few seconds, but it seemed to take an age for him to answer. People were starting to sing *Why are we waiting* and hammering at the front door, frightening Marc who was starting to cry.

95

'I want my mummy,' he said. 'I wish she was here.'

At last Kevin Mitchell answered, promising he wasn't too far away.

'But Mitch, there's so many out there. And I'm frightened they'll try to break in.'

'Sit tight, Mrs Warrender, and whatever you do, don't open that door. I'm calling the cops and I'll be with you in ten.'

For Nanou, the minutes until he arrived seemed to take forever but, as it turned out, the party-goers were not unreasonable kids and wanted no trouble with either Mitch or the local police who quickly convinced them to leave. Without exception, they all told the same tale. A party at *Warrender* had been advertised on the net.

'But who would do such a thing?' Nanou said to Mitch, as she comforted Marc who was still upset and shaken by the occasional sob. 'Just to frighten an old woman and a little boy?'

'People don't really think at all,' Mitch said. 'But I'll spend the rest of the night downstairs in case anyone else turns up.'

'Thank you, Mitch.' The old lady gave him a wan smile. 'It is a great comfort to have you here, after all.'

'And I think we should call Mr Sandford. He said I was to let him know if the slightest thing went wrong.'

'No, please!' Nanou grasped his arm. 'The people have gone now and no harm done. They've just won a prestigious race up there and will have gone out to celebrate. I don't want to spoil the evening for them.'

Reluctantly, Mitch let her persuade him to leave it. But she could see he wasn't happy to do so.

CHAPTER SIX

It didn't take Paige long to realize that Luke wasn't taking the fastest route back to Melbourne. Instead of heading inland towards the Hume Highway, he was driving south along the more picturesque Grand Pacific Drive which would lead them through Wollongong and on to a meandering journey along the coast.

'Have patience,' he said, in answer to her enquiring glance. 'We're taking the long way home because there's something I want you to see.'

Paige sat back and sighed contentedly, giving herself up to admiring the view and relishing the fact that he wanted to prolong their journey. While she loved Melbourne, secure in its olde worlde grandeur and sometime Victorian austerity, a visit to Sydney always lifted her spirits. Although it was a major city as well as a place of business, the beautiful harbour and beaches contributed a light-hearted holiday atmosphere that no one could resist.

In order to make the most of this sojourn with Luke, she had promised herself she would not be distracted or let herself think about anyone else. Not Julia, not Nanou, or even her little son, Marc. *This is our time* Luke had said and, however little that might turn out to be, she was determined to make it count.

Last night although exhilarated by winning The Golden Slipper, they were both too exhausted and wrung out emotionally to make the effort to go out. After accepting the congratulations of the hotel's managers and staff, which included a huge bunch of flowers for Paige, they were finally allowed to go up to their suite where they made their peace with each other and ordered a Chinese take-away. Luke had been so attentive, holding her with the intensity of his gaze, that any barriers, real or imagined, simply ceased to exist.

Having ordered their supper to be delivered, they stepped out of their clothes and showered together, enjoying the feel of warm water cascading over their bodies as they made love joyously, delighting in each other as they celebrated their winning of the race. Afterwards, relaxed and happy, they sat around in the hotel's dressing gowns and drank wine from the bar fridge, waiting for their food to arrive.

It was only as Paige smelled the delicious Asian feast that she realized she was starving, having had little to eat all day. There was a dish of scallops and mushrooms along with bean shoots and other Chinese vegetables, fried rice and a double portion of sweet and sour prawns. Luke had also had the foresight to order a bottle of champagne to go with it.

Having had no time for more than a snack all day, they were both so hungry, they said scarcely a word as they fell upon the fragrant seafood dishes. At last Paige set her chopsticks aside and sat back in her chair, closing her eyes.

'That was fantastic,' she said. 'Maybe the best Chinese food that I've ever tasted.'

'It's the company.' He smiled wickedly. 'Look, there's still a prawn left.'

'You have it.' She blew out a long sigh. 'I couldn't eat another thing.'

Luke quickly disposed of the rest of the meal and then rose to open the drawer of the desk and take out a small parcel, gift wrapped and tied with gold ribbon which he solemnly presented to Paige.

'This is for you,' he said. 'A special thank you for winning the Slipper for me and for being so fabulous in every way. It's all I can do to show my appreciation right now.'

You could say that you loved me. Paige thought, at the same time inwardly cursing herself for a fool. Having made a pact with her conscience to enjoy the rest of this weekend with no thought to the future, there should be no room for regret.

'Go on, open it,' he said.

Inside the wrapping was a black and gold bottle of perfume, bearing the exotic name of *Black Orchid.* She had never been given such a large bottle of perfume before.

She glanced up at him, not knowing what to say. 'It's lovely, I'm sure,' she murmured. 'But fragrance isn't something I usually wear.' Having said this, she looked down at the bottle in her hands, feeling awkward and as if she were being treated like a mistress – which of course, she reminded herself, she was.

'Come on.' He seemed impatient with her hesitation. 'Aren't you going to try it?'

'Oh – um – yes.' Cautiously, she unfastened the cap and sprayed a tiny amount on the inside of her wrists. Then she put a finger to this dampness and dabbed a little behind her ears. The perfume was unusual, putting her in mind of distant tropical islands and exotic flowers – sensual and sexy rather than sweet, and clearly very expensive.

99

'That's no good,' he said, almost roughly. 'I want you to reek of it.' And, before she realized what he would do, he pulled aside her robe and sprayed it all over her. Paige sneezed.

'Oh, Lord,' he said, instantly contrite. 'I'm such a fool. You're not allergic to perfume, are you?'

'No.' She shook her head, laughing weakly. 'But the first notes always do that to me. Strong smells make me sneeze.' And, as if to confirm it, she did so yet again.

'You do like it, though?'

'When I get used to it, yes.'

Soon after that, they turned off the lights and went to bed, leaving only a couple of lamps to enhance the romantic mood. Naked beneath the sheets, they lay kissing and teasing each other with a miasma of Black Orchid wafting around them. As Paige was already saturated with the fragrance, it soon rubbed off on Luke. She decided it smelled even better on him, making her greedy for him which had probably been his intention all along. Not for the first time, she began to wonder about his past. So far he had revealed very little, apart from what she already knew – that he had lived overseas for some time. What exotic tastes might he have developed there? She was starting to understand what Nanou meant by *Indigo Nights*.

'Tell me your fantasies, Luke,' she whispered, in a voice husky with passion. They were now sitting up and she was crouched behind him, kneading a knot of strain in his shoulders. She leaned in, teasing him with her nakedness, by no means unaware that this would arouse him again. 'You have only to say what you'd like.'

'Just keep doing that,' he murmured, giving himself up to her ministrations and closing his eyes. 'You have no idea how good it feels.'

'What do you mean? The massage or the teasing?' she whispered in his ear, before nipping the lobe and making him shiver.

'Both,' he said, luxuriating in her touch a moment longer before reaching for her and drawing her into his arms. She gave a small shriek as he surprised her by turning her over and, kneeling behind her, pulled her into his embrace and swiftly entered her from behind. She closed her eyes, giving herself up to sensation, astonished by her own response to this earthy method of lovemaking. She could feel his every movement inside her and responded, tipping her head back towards him so that he could kiss her shoulders and neck before they finally succumbed to an orgasm that left them both shivering and breathless. Neither of them had any energy left to speak as they collapsed in a tangle of arms and legs, laughing weakly as their breathing returned to normal. Sleep claimed Luke almost immediately but Paige lay awake beside him for quite a while, wondering if after all there might be a future for them together with Julia gone.

For Paige, this visit to Sydney had a dream-like quality, as if even winning the Slipper wasn't quite real. Everything seemed just too perfect. Was this indeed the very best night of her life and the spiral would only be downhill from now on? Would she ever again feel quite so fulfilled, so ridiculously happy? She couldn't help wishing for time to stand still and these golden moments never to end.

And now here they were on the coast road, taking the slower route home.

Although she would have liked to stop now and then to admire the scenery with the ever-changing and spectacular colours of sky and sea – each little bay like a picture post-card – Luke had other ideas. Once clear of Sydney, he didn't dawdle, seeming anxious to get on with the journey. She would have liked to stop and soak up the ambience of some of the small coastal towns on the way but he seemed impatient to push on, stopping only to refuel the car and to buy soft drinks and sandwiches for them to eat on the way.

'Where are we headed?' she said at last, unable to stand the suspense.

'Merimbula on the Sapphire Coast. It's exactly halfway between Sydney and Melbourne. We've made good time today and should be there before nightfall.'

As it happened, they weren't. It was already dark when they pulled up outside a pretty, split-level home with an imposing *For Sale* sign posted outside it.

'Not exactly a shanty on the beach,' Paige said. 'And why are we here? Are you thinking of buying it?'

'No,' he said. 'It's already mine. It belonged to my parents. They moved up here some time ago when they retired. My father came here for the fishing and after he died, my mother decided she loved it enough to stay on. I wanted her to come back to Melbourne, but she said it was too much like Europe and she'd had quite enough of the changeable weather. My son loved it here and it was always her intention to leave it to him.' He sighed and shrugged. 'Sadly, that wasn't to be. I was the only one left to inherit it when she died.'

'Then that must have happened quite recently?' Paige felt tears of sympathy welling as she touched his arm. 'Oh, Luke.'

'No. It was over a year ago now. But it's such a lovely place – I find it hard to let it go.'

'So why are you selling it? Not because you need the

money, surely?'

He shrugged. 'Not really. But Julia said it was too far away for us to make any real use of it. She said we should consolidate our assets in Melbourne.'

Julia again. In spite of Luke's assurances that it would soon be over between them, Paige could see no real evidence that this was the case. She sensed that Julia still loomed large in his life and felt the woman's influence reaching towards them even without her physical presence.

'You're chilled. Let's get inside,' Luke said, misinterpreting her change of mood as he unlocked the door. 'Might be a bit stuffy as it has been closed up with no one living here for some time. The agents have keys but there hasn't been much interest as yet. It's too far for commuters and the garden's too large for the average holidaymaker who just wants a cabin to crash in close to the beach.'

He gave her a quick tour of what she could see at once was a comfortable, open plan home. It had two spacious bedrooms with adjoining bathrooms and there was a third bedroom that Luke said his father had used as a study. Finally, they sat down in the large lounge overlooking the sea.

'You can't really see it right now,' he said, 'but in daylight the views are spectacular from almost every window in the house. But we don't have to stay here if you'd rather not. We can book into a motel?'

'No, no. I love it here,' Paige insisted. 'Much more like home than some impersonal motel. We'll just need a few groceries, that's all.'

'No, we don't,' he said. 'This is a holiday place. There are cafés open all hours. And wonderful restaurants, too. I'm looking forward to showing you some of my favourites.'

'You really do love this place, don't you? I don't think you should part with it,' she added on impulse.

A slow smile spread across his face. 'Thank you for saying that, because I don't really want to. I feel close to my parents and to my son here.'

'And anyone with a soul can see why.' She didn't care that she was implying that Julia was soulless. 'You feel just the same way about it as I feel about *Warrender*. For you, it's much more than a house, it is a beloved family home.'

'You always see things so clearly, Paige,' he murmured. 'I just wish—'

Gently, she touched a finger to his lips. 'Don't wish for anything more than we have here and now. As you said before – this is our time. Shall we make up a bed before we go out?'

Having found sheets and made up the bed in the second room as Luke wouldn't sleep in the bed that his parents had shared, it was tempting to get into it and forget about supper.

'No.' Paige wasn't to be diverted. 'And, before we have dinner, we're buying some groceries, too. I shall want coffee and a fried breakfast in the morning.'

Luke didn't argue but followed her round the small local supermarket which stayed open late. As well as coffee, bread, mushrooms, bacon and eggs, she bought some fruit juice, butter and marmalade. Everything they would need for a wholesome breakfast. Only then would she let him drive her to his favourite restaurant on the wharf.

It was a typical seaside restaurant, decorated with dried starfish, glass balls hanging in nets and old fishing equipment pinned up on the walls. Luke was greeted like an old friend by Tim Foster, the balding, middle-aged owner, who happened to be on the door that evening.

'Congratulations!' he said, slapping Luke on the shoulder. 'I had a feeling you'd win. Put fifty each way on Happy Rosie myself.'

'Good for you.' Luke returned his friend's punch on the shoulder before drawing Paige close to be introduced. 'You should congratulate this young lady, too. She is Paige McHugh – the jockey who steered my horse in to win.'

'Brilliant girl.' Tim gave her a dramatic air kiss. 'You shall have a bottle of champagne on the house.'

Still offering extravagant compliments, Tim showed them to one of his best tables and recommended the local oysters to start with.

'Merimbula is famous for the oysters. So fresh' – he made a kissing gesture with the tips of his fingers – 'you'll need nothing more than a squeeze of lemon and chilli sauce to bring out the flavour.' To follow, he offered them local crayfish, also freshly caught. 'We keep them swimming,' he said, indicating a large aquarium at the back of the restaurant. 'Until we pop them in the pan, of course.'

'Oh no.' Paige shielded her eyes. 'I love crayfish but I can't bear to think of eating someone I've met.'

'Leave it alone, then. Stick to plain old fish and chips,' Luke teased.

'No.' Paige sat down with her back to the aquarium. 'I came to have crayfish and that's what I want. It'll be all right so long as I don't see him struggling on the way to the kitchen.'

'Little hypocrite,' Luke laughed, although he ordered the same.

The oysters were exceptional, just as Tim promised, and the crayfish served warm with a light, cheese sauce and a green salad on the side. 'Tim's special recipe,' Luke confided as he poured her a generous glass of chardonnay to go with it before she could put her hand over her glass. She was feeling quite intoxicated already from their present of champagne which they had been drinking while waiting for their meal to arrive.

They had no room for more than a small serving of ice cream to follow and, while they were eating this, Luke's mobile rang, intruding on their happy mood.

'Who can that be?' he muttered. 'I left a message for the office, telling them to manage without me until after Tuesday and – oh!' He grimaced slightly as he looked at the phone and saw who it was. 'Sorry, Paige. I'd better take this.'

She inclined her head in agreement and he turned slightly away from her.

'Yes, Julia? How are you?' he said, and listened for a while. 'Now calm down,' he said at last. 'Of course everything's all right. I'm sorry if you had a wasted journey and that you were worried, but I didn't expect you to pick me up at the airport. We never arranged it. I cancelled my flight out of Sydney and I'm coming back by road. The coast road.'

Unable to help overhearing, Paige realized he had neglected to tell her he wasn't alone. At this point Julia seemed to have a lot more to say and Luke waited patiently until she ran out of steam and allowed him to speak.

'Yes, but since I was up here anyway, I thought I'd come back via Merimbula and take a look at the house.' He closed his eyes and winced as this produced yet another volume of words from Julia. 'I don't know. I haven't seen the agents as yet, but, far as I know, there hasn't been a firm offer.' He listened again and sighed. 'No, Julia, I don't want to take it away from these agents; they're good people. Reliable. And you might as well know, I'm changing my mind. Thinking of taking it off the market altogether.' This produced such a stream of invective from Julia that he held the phone away from his ear. 'Julia, please stop. This isn't the time or the place to discuss this. I'll see you in a day or so. We'll have a lot to talk about when I get home.' So saying, he snapped the phone shut without even saying goodbye although he continued to stare at it in his hand as if he were afraid she'd ring back.

At last he returned his gaze to Paige, seeing her worried frown. 'Don't look so tragic,' he said, leaning across the table to take her hand and rubbing his thumb across her fingers. 'Julia likes to stir things up and get everyone else going, making a huge drama out of nothing. She's well known for it.'

Paige didn't want to talk about Julia so she forced a smile and tried to return to where they had been and recapture their celebratory mood but the moment was gone. Luke seemed to sense this, too, as he stood up, motioning for Paige to accompany him as he went to find Tim to thank him once again for the gift of champagne, pay the bill and ask if it was all right to leave the car overnight in his car-park. Although home wasn't far away, he didn't think he should drive.

'Always happy to see you, Luke,' his friend smiled. 'Especially with such a pretty young lady in tow.' He lowered his voice to speak confidentially. 'What happened to—? Oh, never mind. Can I book you both in for lunch tomorrow?'

'Unfortunately, no. We'll have to hit the road early if we want to get back to Melbourne by nightfall.'

'But you can't mean to leave already.' Tim's face fell. 'Paige hasn't seen a fraction of what Merimbula has to offer. Go on. Stay one more night at least.'

Paige held her breath, all too aware that Luke had omitted

to tell Julia that she was accompanying him on this journey south.

He hesitated a moment, then he let his shoulders slump and relaxed. 'Oh hell, why not?' He grinned at Tim. 'It's only putting off the evil hour, but I might as well be hanged for a sheep as a lamb. So, yes. Book us in for lunch and we'll set off afterwards.'

Beset by gloomy thoughts about Julia, Paige didn't feel like going straight back to the house, deciding she needed some air. 'Can we take a look at the beach?' she asked. 'I love to hear the waves rolling in to the shore – the sound of the sea always soothes me.'

'And are you in need of soothing, Paige?' His dark eyes looked down into hers finding them sombre and troubled. He took her hand, linking his fingers with her own, as they strolled in the direction of home and the beach. 'Something's not right, is it? Come on, out with it.'

She looked into his eyes for a moment, a swift denial on her lips, until she decided it was better to tell him the truth. 'It's just. . . .' She hesitated, trying to find the right words. 'I'm not entirely comfortable with this role. Of being the other woman.'

'You're not.'

'So what else would you call me?'

His expression clouded. 'Do we have to get into this right now?'

As they arrived at the beach, Paige took off her shoes and trotted towards the ocean, leaving him behind. 'Of course not,' she called back over her shoulder. 'There's plenty of sand here for you to bury your head in.'

He caught up with her in a few quick strides and spun her to face him. She held her breath for a moment, not knowing what would happen. Clearly, she had angered him. Then he bent his head and kissed her roughly, demandingly, almost lifting her off her feet. He didn't stop until they were both breathless and panting.

'There!' he said at last. 'Does that clear up any doubts that you have of my feelings?'

'Well, no. But you can't solve all our problems with kisses, Luke,' she said, feeling emotionally drained as she leaned against him. 'You didn't even tell Julia we were travelling together.'

He laughed shortly. 'And open a whole new can of worms? No. We had enough to argue about without getting into all that. Look, Paige, I really don't want to talk about Julia. You know how things are between us. I'll handle it when we get back to Melbourne. You'll have to trust me on this.'

'Luke, I'm trying to, but you don't make it easy for me.'

To change the subject, Luke picked up a shell and held it to his ear before passing it over to her.

'Listen,' he said. 'You can hear the sea.'

'I can't tell which it is,' she said. 'The sound of the sea in the shell or the real sea itself out there.' She ran to the water's edge, watching the tiny ripples come in. 'The water's so clear and so beautiful,' she said. 'Marc would just love it here.'

'Our beaches are famed for their safety,' he told her. 'Perfect for children. No nasty surprises.' He caught her to him and they engaged in another deep and satisfying kiss. When they finally broke free, Paige was warmed by the intensity and the passion in his gaze. *It will be all right –* she tried hard to convince herself. *It just has to be.*

At around 10.30 that same evening, the telephone started ringing at *Warrender*. Nanou answered it quickly. She didn't want Marc to wake and get out of bed, expecting it to be Paige. She'd had quite enough trouble pacifying him after the last time she rang. The caller wasn't his mother but a woman whose voice she didn't recognize.

'Oh, hello,' The woman's tone was ingratiating, setting Nanou's teeth on edge. 'Sorry to trouble you, but I'm a journalist with the new racing magazine and I was hoping to speak to Paige if she's there? To congratulate her on winning the Golden Slipper—'

Nanou felt an additional frisson of annoyance. 'Have you any idea what time it is? Do you usually intrude on people this late on a Sunday night?'

'Oh, is it that late? So sorry. But journalism never sleeps – we have a deadline to meet. I was hoping to score an in-depth interview with the jockey who won the Slipper?'

'Well, you'll have to wait. She's returning from Sydney by road and I don't know how long it will take. But if you'd care to give me a name and a contact number, I'll get her to—' Nanou broke off, realizing she was talking to a dial tone. 'Really,' she muttered. 'Some people have no manners, these days.' Still shaking her head, she went back to the Jane Austen drama she was watching on television and the whole incident slipped from her mind.

On Monday morning Paige came down to earth as reality kicked in. Used to rising early to exercise horses, she was awake long before Luke who was even now sleeping peace-fully, completely relaxed as he lay on his back, his arms flung up over his head. When daylight came, she continued to watch him, thinking how much younger he looked when he was asleep. This was the last day they would spend on this stolen holiday. Tomorrow night they would be back in Melbourne and they would go back to their usual roles. Julia would reclaim him and this time together would fade to become no more than a memory.

Finding this thought too painful to contemplate, she sat up, hugging her knees and hiding her face against them.

'Paige?' He was awake in an instant, sensing her anguish. 'Whatever's the matter now?'

'Nothing.' She looked up and smiled, determinedly hiding her tears. 'I was just feeling guilty about Marc. We've never been parted this long.'

'Of course.' He accepted the lie and sat up, placing an arm around her. 'We don't have to go back to Tim's for lunch. We can press on after breakfast and get home tonight if that's what you want?'

'No, no.' She couldn't bear to think of losing even a moment of this precious time. 'I'm being silly, I know. I'm sure Marc is all right.'

The making of breakfast together was quite domestic and while Paige washed up, he called the agents asking them to take the house off the market. From his side of the conversation, she could tell they were far from pleased.

'I'm sorry,' he said. 'And I realize there are expenses to be paid. But the house has been available for over six months and with the market as it is now—' He listened for a few moments. 'Yes, I know what Ms Canning said and I don't want you to think I'm ungrateful.' He glanced at Paige and smiled. 'But my circumstances have altered now and I've decided to keep it. And yes, if I want to let it as a holiday home, I will keep you in mind. So, if you'd make it a priority to have your *For Sale* notice removed? This morning, if possible? Thanks. And yes, I'll call by your office before I leave to settle the bill.' He snapped his phone shut and grinned at Paige. 'They weren't happy, but it was easier than I thought.'

He became aware that Paige was no longer listening to

what he was saying as her attention was held by a morning television show which was going out live. He glanced at it with only mild interest until he realized that the blonde hostess was interviewing none other than Julia Canning. Julia, perfectly groomed and made up to the nines as usual, was looking self-satisfied, almost smug.

'And so Julia, where do the boys go from here?' The hostess indicated the band of scruffy young men who were yawning and scratching their heads, resentful of having to show themselves in public at this hour of the morning. They were only grateful they hadn't been asked to sing.

'San Francisco and then home.' Julia said, sounding bright and upbeat as possible to make up for their lethargy.

'And you don't go with them?'

'Heavens no. I'm only in charge of their Melbourne visit.' She glanced at them, unimpressed with what she saw. 'Besides' – she lowered her voice and confided – 'I have a wedding to arrange.' She paused to give her words greater effect. 'My own.'

'How very exciting.' The hostess warmed to this change of subject. 'Where and when is this going to be?'

'Luke – my fiancée – is always busy. For that matter, so am I. You do know he won The Golden Slipper with Happy Rosie? Yes, well I should have been with him but for my business commitments here.' She sighed theatrically, glancing once more at the boys who were now almost somnolent. 'I was so disappointed not to be there to celebrate his moment of glory.'

Luke made an impatient sound in his throat. Paige, appalled yet fascinated, didn't trust herself to say anything.

'Of course,' Julia went on, 'it won't be a surprise for anyone if I announce it on National television but I can't keep it to myself for another moment. Last night Luke said he just doesn't want to wait any longer so we're flying out to Hawaii in three weeks' time to be married in a private ceremony on the beach.'

'Fantastic,' The woman gushed. 'And when all the honeymooning and romance is out of the way, where will you live?'

'Well, Luke has a little place on the Peninsula but it's quite unsuitable for entertaining.' Julia wrinkled her nose. 'More of a farm really where he keeps all his horses. No. I have a wonderful place picked out quite close by – all I have to do now is persuade the owner to sell.'

Paige gasped and, unable to watch any more, Luke killed the television, standing up to pace the room. Paige saw he was coldly furious, white with anger.

'This is so typical of Julia,' he muttered, almost thinking aloud. 'Going ahead and making all these arrangements without telling me.'

'Luke.' Paige could hardly speak through the dryness in her throat. 'You must have said *something*. Something to make her think you're ready for this?'

'The last time I spoke to her was at the dinner table last night. You must have heard what I said?'

'Well, I wasn't trying to, but—'

'I'm sorry, Paige but we'll have to cancel that lunch, after all. I have to get back to Melbourne as soon as possible. I need to see her.'

CHAPTER SEVEN

Although it was the last thing Paige intended to do, she picked a quarrel with him on the way home. In the wake of Julia's announcement, all their happiness, all their triumph and joy in winning the Slipper seemed to be draining away. And, instead of thrashing it out and discussing it reasonably as Paige hoped, Luke retreated into a cold, angry silence, absorbed in his own thoughts and shutting her out. In fact, she wasn't sure who was making him angry – Julia or herself? Perhaps the sight of his fiancée, innocently making plans for their wedding, had jolted him back to reality, forcing him to remember his obligations. Perhaps he even blamed Paige for encouraging him to forget.

After cancelling lunch at Tim's restaurant and leaving Merimbula to bask in yet another golden autumn afternoon, Luke drove with his face set and at a reckless speed until, with brakes squealing, they almost ran off the road at a hairpin bend. Only when he had fought with the wheel and brought the vehicle back under control, did Paige feel obliged to speak.

'Luke, I know you're angry, but listen to me. This isn't a sports car and we still have a long journey ahead – some five hundred kilometres. Whether you speed or not, it won't make a difference of more than an hour or so and I have people relying on me. I'd rather not turn up dead.'

'Fine, fine.' He slowed and pulled the car so dangerously off the road, she could see the cliff edge and the dizzying drop beyond it into the sea. 'You think I'm unsafe, huh? OK. Would you like to drive?'

'No, thank you.' She flinched under his penetrating, angry gaze. 'I'm no good at driving long distances.'

'Then you'd better leave it to those who are. Somehow, whatever I do, I'm always in the wrong. We're making this trip home by road because you were scared of flying—'

'Now that's not entirely fair. The real reason is that you wanted to see how things were at Merimbula.'

'All right. But I needed your input. I wanted you to help me decide whether to sell it or not.'

'Why? Why should it matter what *I* think?' She was brutal in her honesty. 'When Julia's still your fiancée and I'm just the hired help.'

He stared at her for a long moment, as if she were suddenly alien, as if she had turned into a stranger that he didn't know.

'Is that it, then? Is that how you really feel? Have you understood nothing of what's been happening here?'

'I understand that we did what we came to Sydney to do. We won The Golden Slipper and gained quite a lot of money and prestige along the way.' And although her inner self was screaming *Don't do this!* – she made it sound calm, even reasonable as she set out to destroy everything that had taken place between them over the past weekend.

'It was good while it lasted, Luke, and I had a marvellous time. For me it was a real 'on location' adventure. But what happens on location stays on location, right? Now we have to come down to earth, return to our normal lives and do what is expected of us.'

'You don't mean this. You're saying these things just to—'

'I was never more serious in my life. You'll do as Julia wants and have your wedding in Hawaii while I. . . .' She hesitated a moment, shaking her head as she swallowed the tears at the back of her throat. 'Will do what I've always done – I'll look out for Marc, Nanou and the horses. I thought I could do this, Luke, but I can't. I can't be a mistress, always waiting in the wings for you to have time for me. I don't have that kind of patience.'

'I've been such a fool,' he muttered. 'You never meant any of it, did you? It was never anything more to you than a fling – an extended one-night stand. I can't believe I was so mistaken in you.'

She shrugged and looked out of the window, struggling to keep her expression bland, knowing that if she dared to look at him, she would break down. 'Chalk it up to experience, Luke. Women are different these days. No longer the shrinking violets they used to be.'

A quick glance at his expression told her she had done a good job. He was thinking the worst of her now. With a few well-chosen words, she had destroyed any possibility of continuing a relationship between them. For good measure, she decided to go one step further.

'And while we're on the subject of home truths, there's something I've been meaning to ask. Something I'd like to know.'

'Ask away.' His expression was grim.

'What happened to Black Centurion? I never heard of him racing again – not after that day?'

'He didn't. I sold him to a bloodstock ranch up near Queensland – Kirkwoods – you might have heard of it.'

She stared at him, aghast. 'That's a bit irresponsible,

116

isn't it? Selling a rogue horse like Centurion to be put to stud?' The devil that rode on her shoulder kept whispering mischief, urging her to press on, keeping him in the wrong. But Luke merely shrugged, refusing to lose his temper or rise to the bait.

'What else could I do with him? Sell him for cat's meat? No. He had good bloodlines and some of his progeny are doing quite well now. Crowds made him nervous, that's all. There was nothing wrong with the horse away from the track.'

It occurred to Paige that he was speaking in the past tense. '*Was*? Is Black Centurion no longer alive?'

'I'm afraid not. He was out in the paddocks and got bitten by a snake. By the time they got to him it was all too late – nothing to be done.'

'Ah.' Paige nodded slowly, feeling that justice had been served. She couldn't say she was sorry. Instead, she changed the subject yet again.

'I do hope,' she said brightly, keeping a smile on her face. 'That our working lives won't be affected by this? I hope you'll still want me to ride for you?'

'Of course I'll want you to ride for me.' This came out as a low growl. 'I don't cut off my nose to spite my face.'

His mouth tightened as he re-started the engine and drove on, this time at a more acceptable speed. He put on a radio station broadcasting a strident, modern opera; a cacophony of screaming valkyries accompanied by an orchestra that seemed to be fighting the singers to see who could make the most noise. After a while, it gave Paige a headache although it made conversation impossible, suiting Luke's mood. In any case, there was nothing further for either of them to say.

Her arrival home was not the triumphant return that

she had anticipated although her heart lifted a little when Marc ran out to greet her, unable to wait for her to get out of the car. She caught him up in a tight embrace, burying her face in his hair to breathe in the smell of him, only now realizing how much she had missed her little boy.

'Mummy, you're squeezing me.' He squirmed in her arms, complaining and turning to look at Luke. 'Hello, Luke,' he said shyly.

'Mr Sandford to you,' Paige corrected automatically.

Luke managed a smile, ruffling the boy's head. 'Luke's OK by me. We understand each other, don't we, old man?'

Without looking at Paige, he unloaded her bag and carried it to the front door where Nanou was standing, ready to greet them.

'Congratulations, you two.' She smiled like a conspirator, not realizing at first there was anything wrong. 'I let Marc stay up late as this is such a special occasion and I've got a bottle of champagne on ice to celebrate—'

'Not for me, I'm afraid.' Luke cut her short, glancing at his watch. 'Thanks all the same, Mrs Warrender, but duty calls and I have to get this car back to the city.'

Where Julia is waiting for you, Paige thought.

'Get a good night's sleep, Paige.' He looked at her for the first time in hours. 'Early start in the morning. We need to get our heads together – plan Rosie's campaign for the spring carnival.'

'So you'll be back in time for track work.' She was trying very hard to sound casual, as if it really didn't matter. 'I'll see you tomorrow, then?'

'Of course.' He looked at her with mild irritation. 'That's what I said.'

'Now, then.' Nanou tackled her as soon as they were

alone and an over-excited Marc had at last been persuaded to go to bed. 'What was all that about? Glum looks, no champagne and you scarcely picked at your supper. As for the frost between you two – I could feel it like a blast from Siberia. Whatever happened?'

Having kept control of her emotions for over twelve hours, Paige finally lost it and burst into tears. Nanou found a box of tissues and waited patiently for her to recover herself sufficiently to speak.

'Did you watch the local morning show on TV today?' Paige said.

Nanou frowned. This wasn't what she expected. 'You know I never watch daytime TV. Such rubbish. Fit only for old people and idlers with too much time on their 'ands.'

Briefly, Paige explained how Julia had used her television opportunity to announce the proximity of their wedding and force Luke's hand. And went on to say how her own foolish pride had allowed her to quarrel with him and ruin whatever they might have had.

'And before you say anything,' she warned her grandmother, as she grabbed a fresh wad of tissues for her streaming eyes and nose. 'I know you're always telling me we're descended from French courtesans but that just isn't me. I can't bear the thought of sharing him – of being no more than a mistress. Oh, I know he wants me, he's more than proved that already, but he's never said that he loves me. Not once.'

'Hmm.' Nanou looked thoughtful when she had finished. 'Early days for that, *chérie*, at the start of a new and fragile romance. Too soon to expect it.'

'It was fragile, all right. It didn't take much to make it shatter like crystal, did it?'

'All the same, I think you have overreacted. It sounds as if he had as much of a shock over that woman's announcement as you did.'

'So why couldn't he talk about it? Confide in me? Instead, he cancels lunch, throws everything into the car and starts driving home like a maniac to get back to Julia.'

'Not to get back to her: I'd say to set her straight.' Nanou was looking at her granddaughter with a critical eye, watching her cry like a child without inhibition. Snivelling and with her face blotched with tears, she looked far from glamorous. 'Not very good at handling men, are you, Paige?'

This wasn't what Paige expected. She opened her eyes to stare at her grandmother in surprise. 'I don't want to manipulate him – Julia does quite enough of that already. I just expect him to be honest and say what he wants.'

'I'd say he already has, but you're too pig-headed to see it. Poor Luke. No wonder he looked so haunted when he left here.'

'How can you support him, Nanou? I thought you'd be on *my* side?'

'I'm always on your side, *chérie*. But when you 'ave to deal with the wiles of a snake like this Julia, you 'ave to be a little slippery yourself. You might've handled the matter with a bit more – finesse.'

'Finesse? Nanou, I know you want to think the best of him but I can see where he's coming from, even if you can't. Like all men, he's hoping to have his cake and eat it.'

'So what do you do? Instead of being the sugar and spice in his life, you have forced him into a decision he wasn't ready to make. Driving him back into Julia's arms.'

Paige sighed. 'I don't think he ever really left them, Nanou.'

Having sold her prestigious Docklands apartment, Julia

retreated to the cramped quarters she had previously occupied over her city office, evicting the tenant who had been hoping to live there for some time. The situation was far from ideal and she had furniture from the other apartment, her dining table and chairs as well as her Chesterfield, stacked to the roof in the spare room. But it comforted her to know she was saving money. A woman who never allowed a setback to throw her, which was largely the reason for her success, Julia felt it wouldn't take long for her to achieve her long-awaited goal of acquiring *Warrender*. And at that same time a chastened Luke would be brought to heel. She couldn't wait to see the look on his face when she pressed the deeds of *Warrender* into his hands, signed, sealed and delivered without any help from him.

Her pleasant reverie was interrupted by an insistent ringing of her intercom bell accompanied by a thunderous knocking at the outside door.

'Who is it?' She answered the phone in quavering tones, seeing that it was already past midnight. There were nightclubs just round the corner and some of her neighbours had complained of riotous behaviour on behalf of the patrons and plate glass windows smashed on the street.

'Open up, Julia, it's me.' Luke was terse and to the point.

'Oh, Luke, what a lovely surprise,' she gushed. 'I didn't expect to hear from you until tomorrow. Come on up.' She released the lock on the door down below and soon heard his quick footstep on the stairs.

He burst into the room to find her dressed in a warm, old-fashioned red dressing gown and clutching a mug of hot chocolate. With her face bare and pallid without its usual mask of make-up, she looked older than her thirty-five years. He scarcely noticed, launching straight into what he wanted to say with no greeting and certainly without any kiss.

'This time, Julia, you've gone too far.'

'Have I?' She was still smiling but her eyes were wary. He knew that look – she was searching for a way to put him in the wrong. 'That's rich, coming from you, Luke. After spending the weekend frolicking with that female jockey of yours.'

'Who told you that?'

'No one. When you cut me off last night with scarcely a word and no thanks for driving out to the airport for nothing, I got to thinking. All it took was a phone call to the old lady at *Warrender* to find out the lovely Paige hadn't come home either. No prizes for guessing where you both were.'

Luke changed his tack, not wanting to get into an argument about Paige. 'I listened to everything you had to say last night – including the abuse – and I'm sorry if you were angry about that wasted journey to the airport. But, as I said at the time, we need to talk – about where we're both going from here.'

'And what could you possibly want to discuss but the plans for our wedding?' Julia was still smiling but her voice was dangerously soft. 'And you can hardly blame me for trying to protect my own interests. I don't know exactly what happened in Sydney but I can guess. You won the Slipper together and the stable girl took her chance and threw herself at your head. OK. These things happen.'

'Don't talk about Paige like that. She is her own woman, that's all – she isn't a whore.'

Julia shrugged. 'I don't care what she is. She isn't important. I'm prepared to overlook this indiscretion so long as it doesn't happen again. But if you're harbouring any idea of breaking our engagement, I'm telling you now – I've no intention of releasing you or returning your ring.' She wiggled the expensive solitary diamond on her left hand. 'Come on, Luke.' She gave him what she hoped was a winning smile. 'We can laugh about this aberration and put it behind us. You must have made a small fortune out of winning the Slipper. Surely, we can spend at least some of it on a lovely Hawaiian wedding?'

'Julia will you stop talking for one moment and listen. Get this through your head. You can keep the ring – I don't want it. But you and I are not getting married – in Hawaii or anywhere else.'

Julia coloured up and her eyes became hard slits. She was breathing heavily and for just a moment, he almost ducked, thinking she was about to throw the hot chocolate, mug and all, in his face. Instead, she set it down carefully with a hand that trembled only slightly.

'You won't get away with this. I'll sue you. Bring an action for breach of promise.'

'Oh Julia, listen to yourself.' He almost laughed. 'You're not some helpless Victorian maiden whose reputation is going to be ruined by a broken engagement—'

'You shan't throw me over. I won't let you. Not for that little gold-digger – no! I won't have it.'

'It's already happened, Julia.' He sighed. 'It's finished between us. But if it makes you feel any better, I'm not going straight from here into Paige's arms. She's no more in love with me than you are. Right now, her little son Marc thinks more of me than she does.'

'Does he, indeed?' Julia murmured. But Luke scarcely heard her as he was already leaving, closing the door softly behind him.

Although Luke had promised to be there, Paige wasn't all

that surprised when he didn't turn up for track work with Rosie the following morning. She herself felt tired and wrung out, having spent the night reliving their last bitter exchange and getting little sleep. Foolishly, she sprayed some Black Orchid on her pillow. It was like rubbing salt in a wound; the perfume made her recall every heart-stopping second of their intimate moments together.

And, on top of everything else, she had gone too far – a simple *I can't do this any more* would have been quite enough. Instead, she had opened the cupboard and let out all the skeletons, fouling the atmosphere between them rather than clearing the air.

She caught up with Gail and Glenda who were already walking some horses, pulling faces behind Ham Peachey's back and complaining of his surliness.

'Just ignore him,' she said. 'Ham's getting old and grumpy. It's nothing new.'

'So why doesn't he do us all a favour, retire and take himself off?' Glenda frowned at the old man who was even now giving some grief to one of the stable boys.

'If a horse drops a shoe, you bring it right back at once,' he yelled. 'You don't just keep walking.'

'You see?' said Paige. 'He means well. He really does care for the horses. And anyway, this is his home. He has nowhere else to go.'

But the twins looked unconvinced.

Luke was absent for the entire week. Although he made no contact with Paige, she heard indirectly that there were problems with some of his other business interests, claiming his time. By registered mail he sent her a generous cheque which was much more than she had expected for her part in winning the Slipper. In any other circum-

124

stances, it would have delighted her. Instead, she had the sensation of being paid off. At least Nanou was pleased, finally engaging someone to fix the roof before winter really set in.

Paige did just what she told him she would do. She took care of Marc, Nanou and the horses.

The following Sunday night, a thick fog came in from the sea bringing with it a world of eerie silence. Although Nanou and Marc seemed content to toast crumpets over a blazing fire, Paige couldn't shake a feeling of impending menace. But the evening passed without event and by ten o'clock, they were all asleep in their beds.

At midnight, Paige started awake to the roar of more than one motor-bike. At the same time a rock hit one of the downstairs windows, shattering it and setting off the alarm. Marc came running in to her bedroom crying with tears streaming down his face.

'Mummy, Mummy! It's those big boys again. They came back!' He sobbed as she caught him in her arms, murmuring words of comfort and promising, although her own heart was hammering in her chest, that everything was going to be all right.

Cautiously, without putting the light on, she peeked through the curtains to see at least half-a-dozen leather-clad figures on motor bikes looming out of the fog to churn up the lawn and the flower gardens. Like a small army, they wore identical black helmets concealing their faces. If Nanou's rose bushes had already been pruned, they might have escaped their attention but, as it was, they represented an easy target, to be smashed to the ground, scattered or ploughed up by the roots.

With Marc in her arms, she ran to Nanou's room to find

the old lady awake and already talking to Kevin Mitchell by phone.

'But please be careful how you deal with them, Mitch,' she was saying. 'This time it's not just kids looking for amusement. These men are aggressive; they've already smashed a window downstairs and ripped up half the garden. They mean business this time.'

'He's coming at once,' She told Paige. 'And calling the police.'

'I'll call them, too, to make sure.' Paige hurried to do so although she was frowning and looking thoughtful when she came off the phone.

'They say there was trouble here last week while I was away,' she said, holding her son close. He was clasping his arms tightly around her neck and she could feel him trembling, burying his face in her neck to hide from the noise. 'Why didn't you tell me before?'

'Because it wasn't like this.' Nanou was trying not to watch the destruction of her beloved garden. 'Just some kids who got lost on their way to a party.'

By now, Kevin Mitchell had arrived in his van although there was still no sign of the police.

'Attention! Attention!' He addressed the riders through a loudhailer, leaning out of his van. 'Leave at once! Leave now! The police are on their way.'

He might have saved his breath. The only response was from one of the riders who picked up a rock from the garden to hurl at him. Mitch ducked and it went wide, missing him and shattering his windscreen instead.

Sirens and flashing blue and red lights loomed out of the fog on the main road heralding the arrival of two police cars. Responding to a signal from their leader, the riders, in almost military formation, sped off into the night, making use of the fog for concealment, taking care to be long gone before the police arrived. One of the police cars took off in pursuit of them, while the other one came down the drive to *Warrender* to find out what was happening at the house.

Leaving Nanou in the kitchen to make a drink of hot milk for Marc, Paige ran outside to speak to Mitch and make sure he was unhurt. She found him brushing pieces of his shattered windscreen from his hair.

'I'm so sorry, Paige.' He stared at the broken downstairs window and ruined garden surrounding it. 'I haven't been much use to you, have I?'

'It would have been a lot worse without you,' she said. 'Not much you can do against somebody this determined to scare us.'

'You know who's behind it all, then?'

'I have no proof as yet. But I do have a good idea. A person determined to frighten my grandmother into selling her house.'

'If you have any suspicions at all, you should mention them to the police.'

Paige shook her head. 'Not yet. I have to be certain. I'll look a prize fool if I'm wrong.'

'Better to look a prize fool than have anything like this happen again. And it's escalating – getting worse. Last week Mrs Warrender wouldn't let me tell Mr Sandford said it was just kids on a prank. This time, I'll have to give him a full report.' He nodded towards the broken window. 'And aside from Mrs Warrender's roses, you've got property damage this time.'

CHAPTER EIGHT

Luke arrived at *Warrender* shortly after 8.30 a.m the following morning He rang the front door bell hesitantly, unsure of his welcome.

But Mrs Warrender greeted him warmly, showing him the last night's damage with a rueful smile. 'And look at my poor old roses. Some of them were past their best and I was thinking of replacing them. But I'd rather have dealt with it in my own time.'

'Senseless vandalism,' Luke muttered. 'As if someone's picking on things that are precious to you, just to cause hurt.'

'Yes, it's hard to believe.' The old lady looked troubled, hearing these words. 'We live quietly here and, far as I know, we've made no enemies.'

'I don't mean to frighten you but I'd say you have a very determined enemy here. Mitch tells me this wasn't the first unpleasant nocturnal visit you had?'

'That's right, but I'm not even sure these incidents are connected. And I'd certainly rather not think so.' Mrs Warrender shivered and tossed her head as if to dispel the disquieting thought. 'But let's go inside and have coffee. It's freezing out here.' Expecting Luke to follow, she led the way into the house.

He hesitated a moment before following her, preparing himself to be pleasant and casual with Paige. Crazily, he felt a pang of disappointment when he discovered she wasn't there.

'So where did Paige go?' he said, stirring sugar into a cup of Mrs Warrender's strong coffee as they sat companionably at the kitchen table. 'Not that I really expected her after what happened last night. But she's usually there, rain or shine – so I wondered—?'

'I'm not sure.' The old lady frowned. 'Seemed a bit secretive about it, too. Said she needed to go to the city and she'd drop Marc off at play school on the way. Seemed distracted, not like herself at all. I think she's up to something.'

'Maybe she wanted to call at the office and see the insurance people in person?'

'Then why didn't she say so, if it was only that?'

Luke stood up and pushed his chair back in place at the table. 'Well, it's good to see you're OK, Mrs Warrender, and thanks for the coffee. But I really do have to dash.'

'Call me Nanou, Luke. Everyone else does around here. And please, would you sit down and give me a moment more of your time? There's something I'd like to ask you while Paige isn't here.'

Having no idea what the old French lady might want, Luke became wary. But, obediently, he sat down at the table again and allowed her to pour him a fresh cup of coffee.

'Fire away,' he said. 'I'll answer you honestly, if I can.'

'So tell me. What happened in Sydney to upset things between you two?'

Luke's eyes widened in surprise. He wasn't accustomed

to such direct questions from elderly ladies. Without waiting for him to fabricate a slick answer, she went on,
'Because when I spoke to Paige after winning the Slipper,
she couldn't have been more happy or thrilled – on your
behalf as much as her own. What happened to spoil all of
that? Something to do with your fiancée, perhaps?'

'Mrs um – Nanou – you're crossing the line here. I really
don't think I should be talking about this behind Paige's
back.'

'You slept with her, didn't you?' she said. Her tone wasn't
accusatory, more like a statement of fact. Luke took a deep
breath, but still didn't speak. 'Well, it's admirable that you
don't like to kiss and tell, but you should know that this
isn't something Paige would do lightly. She's not in the
habit of collecting men friends, whatever she might have
led you to believe.'

'OK,' he said. 'But I still don't think we should be
discussing this.'

'Why not? Who else is there to look out for my granddaughter? Paige and Marc are all I have in the world – all
I care about. Nothing matters to me except those two – and
the people they care about, of course.' She peered at him,
studying his bleak expression. 'You don't look so good yourself, Luke. Have you had any breakfast?'

'No. And not much sleep last night after talking to Mitch.
I wanted to come over right away, but he said it would be
best to leave it till morning.'

'If you haven't slept, you must eat instead. I'll cook something for both of us. And you can stop fidgeting and looking
at your watch. You're not going anywhere until you've had
your breakfast and listened to what I have to say.'

He smiled. 'You can be quite a bully, can't you? And I
thought you were such a sweet old lady.' All the same, he

relaxed and helped her to prepare breakfast, watching the toast and buttering it when it was done. It reminded him all too vividly of that last morning in Merimbula, making breakfast with Paige.

Nothing but small talk passed between them until they had finished their meal. Luke hadn't realized how hungry he was until she set it before him. Nanou made a fresh pot of coffee and poured it for both of them. Only then did she sit back, ready to speak.

'To understand Paige, you need to know of her history. Did she tell you her parents were aid workers in Africa?'

'No. She never mentions them.'

'Well, she was very small when they died. They were in the wrong place at the wrong time and got themselves killed, leaving Paige to be brought up by me. And then Ruary came on the scene. My, how we fought over him; I handled it badly and nearly lost her completely. They didn't have a proper wedding at all – no bridesmaids and no pretty dress. They just ran away and got married in front of some marriage celebrant that Ruary knew. They only told me when it was— How do you call it?' Nanou hesitated, trying to find the right expression. 'A done deal. I knew all along he would make her miserable but she married him anyway. And then came that awful day he was killed on the track—'

'Yes, I know all about that.' Although Luke felt awkward about it, he felt bound to say. 'He was riding my horse.'

'So. There was Paige left a widow, already carrying Marc.'

'Mrs – Nanou – I'm sorry to interrupt you but this is old news. Do we really have to go over all this again?'

'Absolutely. If you want to understand Paige. I'm sorry if it makes you uncomfortable.'

Luke shrugged, staring into his coffee cup.

131

'If only Ruary had been different – a faithful husband – it might not have hurt her so much. She could have grieved for a while and then kept him as a golden memory. Instead, we had a parade of his girlfriends – one even turned out for his funeral – making Paige feel foolish as well as betrayed.'

'I see,' he said slowly.

'I hope you do, Luke. Because that experience so damaged her, it made it doubly hard for her to trust another man.'

'All right, I'll tell you. She seemed to be brooding and then suddenly, on the way home, she threw up all the barriers and pushed me away. She said what happened between us in Sydney was just an "on location" adventure – no more than a fling—'

'And do you blame her? After seeing Miss Canning broadcasting her plans for your future together on national television? No wonder she thought she needed to get in first.'

Luke clapped his hands to his head. Then he stood up, came round the table to hug Nanou and plant a smacking kiss on her cheek. 'I was so angry with Julia, I didn't think to explain. I should've known how it would seem to her. What an idiot I've been.'

'And how do things stand between you and Miss Canning now?' The question was bold and Nanou wasn't at all sure he would answer it but at this stage she thought she had nothing to lose.

'I went to see her at once and told her there won't be a wedding. Our engagement is off.'

Paige, forced to patronize a high-priced car-park in the city, was reconsidering her impulsive decision to confront Julia Canning on home territory in her office. After talking to

132

Mitch, it had seemed the sensible thing to do, making the woman realize she had been found out and warning her off. Now she was actually here, she wasn't so sure. She had dressed carefully in her one good suit, but, as she walked through the city streets on the way to Julia's office, she could see her clothing appeared slightly dated and out of touch. There was a more relaxed look to the girls in the city, these days. The theme was still mainly black but a lot more casual, often relieved with a colourful scarf. Girls wore black footless leggings and flatties instead of sheer black stockings and high-heeled shoes.

Julia's outer office was no less imposing; minimalist and smart with no pictures upon the bare white walls other than an enlarged map of the Melbourne CBD with flags on all the possible venues for concerts and sporting events. A chrome hatstand stood in a corner, hung with the coats and scarves of the people who worked there. She employed a receptionist who was young and far from good-looking as well as an older woman who sat staring at a computer screen and attacking her keyboard as though her life depended on it. Both were dressed in identical long-sleeved white blouses and plain black skirts.

'Miss Canning?' Paige smiled at the receptionist. 'Is she here?'

'She is, indeed.' The girl looked Paige up and down, clearly thinking she didn't look like one of their usual clients. 'Do you have an appointment.'

'No. But I think she'll see me, if you tell her it's Paige.'

'Oh.' The girl's expression cleared. 'You're a personal friend, then. I'll ring through and tell her you're here.'

Paige smiled but she didn't deny this assumption.

After announcing the visitor, the girl's eyes widened at whatever Julia said, giving Paige a reproachful glance. 'You can go in,' she said in a small voice, indicating a corridor off the main office. 'First door on the right.'

'Well, Miss Warrender.' Julia didn't rise to greet her but sat back in her chair, steepling her fingers. 'To what do I owe the pleasure of this visit? Are you here to tell me old lady Warrender has at last decided to sell?'

'No, I'm not.' Paige could feel her temper rising and fought to control it. She would achieve nothing if she allowed the woman to goad her. 'And, by the way, my name isn't Warrender, it's McHugh. I happen to be a widow.'

'So?' Julia shrugged. 'A widow. And there I was thinking you bore your son out of wedlock. So fashionable, these days. What's his name? Marc, isn't it? Little Marc McHugh.' She picked up a pen and doodled on her blotter. 'The name has a nice ring to it. How old is he now? Does he go to school?'

'No. Just the Happy Elves Playschool near home.' Paige heard herself answering through lips that were suddenly stiff. Why on earth had she said that? She really didn't like talking to Julia about her son.

'Well now, isn't that sweet?' Julia was once more doodling on her blotter. 'The Happy Elves – very Enid Blyton.' When she was done she glanced at Paige, head on one side. 'Mrs McHugh – Paige – we both know this isn't a social visit – you haven't come to make small talk about matters of family. And since you're not here to offer the sale of your grandmother's property, maybe you'll state your business quickly and leave. I have a busy afternoon ahead of me.'

Paige took a deep breath and launched into the speech that she had been preparing on her way to town. 'I'm here to tell you that whatever you do, whoever you send to throw stones at our windows and churn up our gardens, we won't be intimidated. We won't let you drive us out.'

'I'm sorry.' Julia's smile was one she might bestow on a harmless imbecile, lips twitching as if she wanted to laugh. 'But you've lost me. I have no idea what you're talking about.'

'Oh, I think you do. I'm talking about the biker gang you sent to terrorize us last night.'

'No, that's too much.' Julia stood up and came to open the door, indicating that it was time for Paige to leave. 'I don't have to sit and listen to such drivel. You're not laying this at my door. Bikers, you say? Whatever makes you think I'd have anything to do with such people – or late-night party-goers? You'd better look elsewhere for your scapegoat. These incidents have nothing to do with me.'

Paige could see she had no option but to leave, feeling that she had achieved very little. All Julia had to do was deny all knowledge of those late night visits and she would be believed. Even to her own ears, the accusations seemed quite preposterous. It was only as she was climbing back into her car and preparing to drive home that it finally came to her. While she herself had mentioned the bikers and the destruction of last night, at no time had she said anything about the party-goers who came while she was in Sydney. And although she still had no real proof, she knew now that Julia must be involved.

Moments after Paige left, Julia barged into her outer office, grabbing her coat from the stand.

'Ms Canning, you're not going out?' Her PA was looking horrified, glancing at the clock. 'Mr Wilkinson and his over-seas visitors are due here in half an hour. You can't have forgotten?'

'Cancel,' Julia snapped. 'I'll be out for the rest of the day.'

'Cancel at this late hour?' The older woman glanced at

the receptionist, hoping for support but the girl avoided her gaze, rummaging in the drawer of her desk. 'And don't forget you have a meeting at four with the—'

'Cancel that, too.' Julia waved impatiently, already striding towards the door.

'But what shall I say?'

'You'll think of something.' Julia's smile was cruel. 'That's what I pay you for. I leave it to your ingenuity – you can tell them whatever you like.' And with that, she was gone.

Not long afterwards, Nanou received a phone call from Jenny at Marc's little school.

'Sorry to bother you, Mrs Warrender, but we're updating our records on the computer and we don't seem to have Mrs McHugh's current mobile number.'

'So why do you need it now? Is anything wrong?'

'No, not at all. We're just making sure our records are all up to date.'

Nanou recited the number and rang off, tutting about the inefficiency of the people at that school.

Although Paige now felt she had something on Julia, the proof was just as elusive as ever. It wouldn't do to make wild accusation she couldn't substantiate. Julia's lawyers would be down on her in an instant, making mincemeat of her if she did. As she drove slowly through the crowded streets, leaving the city, her mobile started to ring. Fortunately, a parking space appeared on her left and she was able to pull over in time to accept the call.

'Paige McHugh.'

'Oh, Mrs McHugh, thank goodness I've found you.' The speaker seemed breathless with agitation as well as quite young. 'It's Jenny here – from the Happy Elves Playschool.

Now please, don't be upset, but Marc's had an accident.'

'Marc?' Paige felt suddenly breathless, as if icy fingers were gripping her heart. 'I – I'm just leaving the city now. I can be with you in less than an hour. Is Mrs Avery there? Can I speak to her now—?'

'No, I'm sorry. That's why she asked me to call you. She's gone to the hospital with Marc.'

'The local hospital?' Paige's heart gave another lurch.

'No – the ambulance took them to Dandenong. They do microsurgery there.'

'Microsurgery?' Fear made her terse. 'What the hell happened to my son?'

'Oh Mrs McHugh, I'm so sorry. We watch the children so carefully all of the time. But he fell off the slide and cut his wrist – it was awful, blood everywhere and all the children were crying.'

Paige closed her eyes against a wave of panic, taking deep breaths to calm herself. She would need all of her wits about her to drive. 'I'm ringing off now, Jenny. I want to get to the hospital quickly. But do call me again if there's any more news.'

'Yes. Yes, I will.' The girl sounded ready to burst into tears herself. 'Poor little Marc. He was so brave.'

Paige felt like crying, too, but she cut the girl short. 'Goodbye, Jenny.'

As she drove in and out of the traffic to reach the hospital in record time, various mental pictures haunted Paige's mind. Marc, a small figure, white against a pile of pillows, ready to die from loss of blood. Marc in an operating theatre with surgeons in green all around him, mending his broken body under bright lights.

She drove right up to the hospital's emergency entrance and got out of her car.

'Hey!' a man called out to her when he saw it. 'That place is for ambulances. You can't park there.'

'Watch me,' Paige said, very tempted to give him the finger but deciding against it. He might have her car towed away. Right now, she didn't care if he did.

She tapped her foot, barely able to conceal her impatience, as she waited to speak to the triage nurse who was dealing with someone who seemed to be slow-witted as well as partially deaf. Finally, the woman was free.

'My son is here – Marc McHugh,' she told the nurse. 'He was brought here by ambulance.'

'When?' The woman consulted her list, looking puzzled.

'I don't know. An hour ago – maybe more. A Mrs Avery would have been with him. Perhaps I can speak to her?'

'Wait here,' the nurse said, 'and I'll see what I can find out.' And she disappeared into the emergency wards behind various curtains. Paige waited, doing her best not to scream with impatience.

Although it was just a few minutes, to Paige it felt like an hour before the nurse came back.

'I'm sorry,' she said. 'But are you sure he was brought to this hospital? I've been here all morning myself and we have no record of a seriously injured child being brought here this morning—'

'Of course it was here. You do microsurgery, don't you?'

'Not without a specialist's opinion and a proper appointment. I'm so sorry, Mrs—?'

'McHugh.'

'But, for us, it has been a quiet morning. We have no one answering to your son's description or the lady who supposedly came with him.'

Seeing there was nothing more to be gained from the hospital, Paige ran back to her car. What was going on? She called the playschool, hoping to talk to Jenny again. This time it was Mrs Avery herself who answered the phone.

'Paige, my dear,' she greeted her kindly. 'What can I do for you?'

'Mrs Avery, did Marc have an accident this morning?'

'Dear me, no. I should have called you at once. You know that.'

'Because Jenny – your assistant – rang to say you'd taken him to the hospital.'

'Jenny? There's no one by that name working here, dear. I can't afford an assistant except a work experience girl now and then.'

'So, what are you saying? That Marc is still there?'

'Oh no, dear. It's lunchtime – well after one. All the children have gone.'

'So, my grandmother must have collected him?' Even as she asked this, Paige knew that she hadn't. It had been arranged that she would pick him up on her way home from the city.

'No, dear. That friend of yours picked him up – he was the last to go.'

'What friend?' Paige was doing her best not to give way to panic and shout.

'She seemed such a nice lady – so well dressed – and driving a silver Mercedes, too.'

'Did you' – Paige swallowed, knowing it was a vain hope – 'did you get the number of her car?'

'Of course not. Why should I do that? She seemed such a lovely lady with pretty blonde hair.'

'So you're telling me my child has been snatched? By a stranger?'

'Oh, I don't think so. Marc knows better than that. A lady policeman comes and gives regular talks to the children about stranger danger.'

'Not that effective – obviously.'

'There's no need to be rude. The lady didn't seem strange to Marc. She gave him an enormous lollipop and he let her take him by the hand. This is just a misunderstanding, surely? Everything will turn out all right.'

Paige snapped her mobile shut, ending the call. She didn't trust herself to say anything more. Holding down her need to give way to panic, she called Nanou. If, by some miracle, Marc was at home, there was no need to alarm her grandmother, too.

'Nanou, did – did somebody bring Marc home for me?' She asked, trying to keep the tremor from her voice.

'Why no, Paige. You said you'd pick him up yourself on your way home. But someone from the school did ring earlier, wanting your mobile number. Why? Is anything wrong?'

Trying not to break down completely, Paige told her grandmother as much as she knew.

'Hold on a minute while I tell Luke. Fortunately, he's still here. We had a late breakfast together.' Paige listened as Nanou filled him in on the details and then he came on the line.

'Paige? What's up? Has something happened to Marc?'

'I don't know, Luke, but I'm afraid he's been kidnapped. Snatched from playschool.'

'Are you quite sure? Have you talked to the people there?'

'Of course. I had this crazy call from a girl who told me she worked there, saying he was at the hospital.' It was just a hoax to keep me busy while – while they took him.'

'I've got the picture now. Have you called the police? Kevin Mitchell?'

'Not yet. I wanted to make quite sure he wasn't at home.'

'All right. You can leave that to me.'

'Oh, Luke, I can't bear it. Most kidnapped children are dead within forty-eight hours.'

'Don't give way to such thoughts.' Luke's tone was grim. 'We're not dealing with anything like that yet. And don't drive like a madwoman but get home as soon as you can.'

CHAPTER NINE

With this new concern over Marc to break down the barriers, Paige set aside her differences with Luke. How trivial they seemed in the light of this new disaster. Luke, in turn, realized there was much to discuss and put right between them but now wasn't the time. Although they both knew it was pointless since Marc had been abducted by car, he drove her all over the countryside searching for him, aware that she needed to get out of the house and take action rather than wait for news at home. He didn't try to engage her in conversation or offer false hopes; he could see it would do no good.

Sunk in a gloomy reverie, Paige was trying to make sense of it all; to understand why someone should want to kidnap her little boy. Maybe this was the price of fame – to do with winning the Slipper? If so, she vowed she would never put herself forward to ride in a major race ever again. But so far there had been no threatening phone calls or ransom notes asking for money. *Please God*, she prayed silently, *just let him come back unharmed.*

Gail and Glenda also joined in the search, taking ponies and riding through the woods and paddocks on either side of Mrs Avery's school. But, as the sun lay low in the sky and the chill of evening informed them night was about to fall, they had to give up and go home. Paige and Luke returned also, only to find that neither Kevin Mitchell nor the police had any more news.

At 5.30, just as Paige was about to give way to a new wave of despair, Marc came home. He just turned up at the back door with a red balloon on a stick, chocolate all round his mouth and pink in the face from being so long out of doors. Unaware of the upheaval that had been caused by his absence, he was grinning as if he'd been having the time of his life.

'Marc, where the hell have you been?' Paige knelt and seized him by the upper arms, relief making her want to shake him. Looking into her troubled face, the little boy's smile faltered.

'Mummy, what is it? What's wrong?' he said in a small voice, his lower lip beginning to tremble.

'Paige!' Nanou snapped, with a meaningful look at her granddaughter. 'No need to make more of this than there is. You come with me, darling,' she said to Marc in a gentler tone. 'I'll give you a bath. We'll get rid of that chocolate face and you can tell me what you've been doing all afternoon.'

'Oh, Nanou. I had such a good time. She was such a nice lady and brought me a lollipop. She said I could go anywhere I liked and I said the petting park. I've been wanting to go there forever and nobody ever has time—'

With a hand clapped over her mouth and fresh tears in her eyes, Paige watched the little boy mounting the stairs with Nanou, still chattering about the happy experiences of his day.

'Oh, Luke,' she said. 'How could I do that? My little boy. I almost hit him for looking so pleased with himself while I've had such a dreadful time.'

143

Luke put an arm around her shoulders and gave her a squeeze. 'Well, you didn't hit him, did you? It's OK. Anyone can see your nerves are in shreds. Just let Nanou deal with him. Right now, she stands a better chance of finding out what he's been up to than you do.'

'But why would anyone do this to us? Why would she go to all the trouble of taking him only to let him go? It doesn't make any sense.'

'Unless she's trying to make a point' Luke said, looking thoughtful again.

At that moment, Nanou returned from upstairs, looking grim. She spoke in a whisper so that her voice wouildn't carry upstairs. 'Marc's still in the bath. And he's fine,' she said in answer to Paige's anxious look. 'But I found this note in the top pocket of his jacket. I thought you should see it.'

It was only a line printed in capital letters and didn't say very much.

YOU SEE HOW EASILY THIS CAN HAPPEN? THINK ABOUT IT.

'It's a warning,' Paige whispered. 'Some kind of threat – that any time she likes, she can take him again. Oh, Luke, what shall I do? I can't watch Marc twenty-four hours a day.'

'And you shouldn't have to,' he said. 'But don't give way to panic. To give us the best chance of nailing this person, we need to think it through calmly. Marc spent the whole afternoon with her – his description might help.'

'Luke, he's just a little boy. Grown-ups all look the same to him!' Paige was almost shouting in desperation, until Nanou put a finger to her lips, heading for the stairs yet again. 'He can't even remember what he had for Christmas, let alone give a description good enough to get this woman arrested.'

'Arrested for what?' Luke said. 'Taking your son to the pet park and showing him a good time? You told me yourself that the playschool lady denies any thought of abduction. Very bad for business.'

'It will be bad for her business all right. I'm taking Marc away.'

'Don't do that. All his friends are there – he'll feel as if he's being punished for something he didn't do. Throw wild accusations around without proof and you'll be the one to look crazy and paranoid.'

'You're not suggesting we should let it pass and do nothing? We'll be like sitting ducks, waiting for it to happen again.'

'No, we won't.' Nanou had come downstairs again with Marc who was already in his dressing-gown, yawning and ready for bed. 'Because I think I know who's behind all this.' She paused, making sure she had their full attention before going on. 'Julia Canning.'

'Oh no, I don't think that's likely,' Luke said, beginning to look at Nanou as if she'd lost her mind. 'First and foremost, Julia's a businesswoman. I can't see her as a criminal. What does she have to gain from kidnapping Marc? And, in any case, how would she know where to find him?'

'Because I told her,' Paige said in a small voice. 'I didn't mean to but somehow she dragged it out of me. She has that effect on people.'

'When was this? When did you see her?'

'Just this morning. I went to her office.'

'You actually went there? Confronting Julia on home territory?'

'Yes. It was a stupid idea – I can see that now. I wanted

to find out if she was behind our unpleasant nocturnal visitors. She had only to take the high moral ground and deny it while I ended up telling her where to find Marc.'

Luke shook his head. 'OK. But I still don't see why she would do it. It doesn't make sense.'

'I think it does,' Nanou broke in. 'We never told you but she came here one evening a few months ago, offering us a ridiculous price for the house—'

'Now that I *can* believe,' Luke said. 'She was furious when I told her it wasn't for sale – she's had a lifelong obsession about the place. Calls it her Shangri-la. Even so, I wouldn't expect her to go to such lengths.'

'Well, it doesn't take much to cause trouble.' Nanou shrugged. 'She certainly had me rattled. So I wave the white flag. I give up. If Miss Canning wants *Warrender* that badly, she can have it. I'd rather say good-bye to my home than see any member of this family in danger.'

'You're not saying good-bye to anything.' Luke's expression was grim. 'I know how to deal with Ms Julia Canning.'

'Don't underestimate her,' Paige said. 'She'll be too slippery for you – like she was for me.'

He pulled her into his embrace and gave her a thoughtful rather than passionate kiss on the lips. 'Paige, I know how hard it is for you to sit tight and do nothing, but this time will you leave it to me? If it really is Julia behind this campaign of terror, will you let me deal with it in my own way?'

'I suppose so,' Paige agreed reluctantly. 'But you will be careful, won't you? She's not right in the head.'

'I know,' he said. 'I can't think why I didn't see it before.'

Although the very thought of spending time with Julia was distasteful to him, he invited her out to dinner, aware that it wasn't her style to make a spectacle of herself in a public place. As he collected her from her office, looking trim in her signature little black dress, professionally made-up and with her most vivid publicity smile, he wondered what he had ever seen in her. Everything about her now set his teeth on edge.

'Isn't it lovely to have everything back to normal again?' she murmured, blowing him an air kiss and settling her matching black pashmina about her shoulders. 'I knew you didn't mean all those terrible things you said.'

'Julia, I—' he began.

'It's all right.' She cut him short, patting his arm. 'It's forgotten already. No need to apologize.'

With a tight smile, Luke opened the door of his car and settled her in the passenger seat, not trusting himself to say anything else.

To avoid the intimacy of conversation in the car, he didn't drive far. Just to a restaurant overlooking Albert Park Lake. If they actually got so far as to eat together, he knew Julia would want steak. Leaving the car to be valet-parked, he ushered her inside where the host almost ran to meet them, greeting them like old friends.

'Mr Sandford – Ms Canning – how lovely to see you again. It's been too long. I've saved you your special table by the window.'

'So good of you. Thank you!' Julia beamed at him, gracious as royalty although she hadn't troubled to remember his name.

'Thanks, Paul,' Luke murmured.

When the wine waiter arrived for their order, Julia asked for a champagne cocktail, pulling a face when Luke ordered a double whisky instead.

'That's not very festive,' she pouted.

147

'Maybe I don't feel very festive,' he growled. She widened her eyes and wriggled her shoulders, for the first time looking less than sure of herself.

'Cheers!' she said brightly when their drinks arrived. 'This is delicious. So refreshing. Aren't you sorry you didn't have one now?'

He answered her by tossing his drink back in two quick gulps, signalling the waiter to bring him another.

'You drink too much.' Julia frowned her disapproval.

'Only when driven to it,' he snapped, through gritted teeth.

'Well, if you're in that sort of mood, you should have stayed home. I thought we were going to celebrate.'

'Celebrate what, Julia? Your kidnapping Paige's little boy?'

'Excuse me?' She drew herself up and stared at him, eyes wide and pressing her hand to her throat as if she were shocked. 'Did I hear that? You're actually accusing me of kidnapping a child?'

'Don't play games, Julia. You know you did. And left a threatening note in his pocket.'

'Oh, all right.' She gave in and sat back in her seat, looking peevish. 'But you have to admit that I did a good job of it. I never realized I was such a good actress, pretending to be some little ditz from the playschool. Getting his mother chasing off to the hospital on a fool's errand. I had plenty of time to meet the child out of school and whisk him away. A demanding little brat he is, too. I stuffed him with ice cream and chocolate and gave him a wonderful time. Then I dropped him off home again. What's so terrible about that?'

'Everything! Paige is a devoted mother. You must have known she'd be out of her mind thinking the worst.'

148

'Oh, yes.' Julia leaned forward on her elbows to smile at him. 'That was my intention.'

It took all his self-control not to lean across the table and slap the smile off her face. 'You evil witch,' he said at last. He spoke only softly but his tone was vehement enough to alert other diners nearby who glanced at them anxiously, realizing they were having a row.

Julia pouted, trying to look injured. 'So I'm a witch now, am I? Just for looking after my own interests. I had to do *something*, didn't I? None of my other strategies worked.'

'Other strategies? I don't know how you can sit there, smiling and admit that you were responsible for paying people to frighten an old lady and a little boy.'

'Well, it was time for the gloves to come off, wasn't it? And I didn't pay anyone. Just threw a few concert tickets around. It doesn't take much. You'd be surprised how people love to get up to mischief.'

'Mischief? Breaking windows and wrecking Mrs Warrender's garden?'

'Yes, it was a shame about that.' Julia wrinkled her nose. 'They got a bit carried away. But the whole garden's going to need landscaping, anyway. We'll need a circular drive.'

'I don't believe I'm hearing this. You're like a medieval baroness, riding roughshod over everyone to get your own way.'

'A medieval baroness?' Julia considered this. 'I take that as a compliment. Maybe in a past life that's what I was. Luke, please try to understand. This was always about *Warrender* and scaring them just enough to persuade the old lady to sell. It has nothing whatsoever to do with *us*.'

'Julia, get this through your head, once and for all: there is no more *us*. Tonight is our swan song. And you can forget about *Warrender* because if you pull any more stunts and cause those people any more grief, you'll answer to me. I have unpleasant friends who like to get up to mischief, too.'

'You wouldn't do that. Not to me!'

'No? This has to stop. Now. Tonight. After that you can go to Hawaii and marry whoever you like, but it won't be me.'

'No!' Julia slapped her hand down on the table, making cutlery and glasses clatter. 'That's not going to happen. I won't let you do this to me.' An angry blush started to spread from her throat as she glared at him, eyes glistening with fury.

'It's already done. We're finished, Julia.' He tossed some money towards her across the table. 'That should cover your meal. Order whatever you like – you'll be dining alone.'

He stood up, placing his hands on the table to steady himself but he wasn't paying sufficient attention. Before he realized what she would do, Julia picked up a pointed steak knife and stabbed him through his right hand, pinning him to the wooden surface of the table. Luke stared at it in astonishment as blood welled up from the wound, shockingly red against the white damask tablecloth. Then the pain kicked in and he sat down heavily, refusing to give her the satisfaction of hearing him grunt in pain.

'I hope that hurts because this is just the beginning,' Julia said as she flung her wrap around her shoulders and stood up to leave. 'You'll pay for this, Luke. I'll make you sorry you ever set eyes on Julia Canning.'

Moments later, she was gone and he was surrounded by concerned waiters, not only anxious to help him but to minimize the effect on the other patrons. So much for his theory that Julia wouldn't cause a scene in a public place. Steeling himself for yet more pain, he pulled the knife out of his hand. Fortunately, her aim wasn't accurate. She had missed sinews and bone entirely, causing only a deep flesh wound in the side of his hand. All the same, it hurt like hell and would probably need to be stitched. He allowed the restaurant manager to usher him to the office where the first-aid kit was kept.

'Are you sure you don't want me to call an ambulance?' he asked Luke. 'You look awfully pale – could be in shock?'

'No,' Luke said. 'Just patch me up enough so that I can get home.'

'You should go to the hospital. Get a tetanus shot.'

Grimacing, Luke agreed, and allowed the man to drive him to the nearest Outpatients' Emergency. It looked like being a long night.

Meanwhile, Julia, shivering in the wind without a coat, was trying to flag down a taxi in the road outside. If it weren't for the scene she had caused, she could have asked the host at the restaurant to summon one and waited inside until it arrived. Too late now. Worse still, it had come on to rain, plastering her hair to her head and chilling her further. More than three taxis passed without slowing down and one even drove through a puddle and splashed her, adding to her discomfort. Another came by and she waved frantically but to no avail. When she was ignored yet again by the driver of that one, she ran out into the road behind it, screaming and swearing in uncontrollable rage. It made no difference. The car turned at the end of the street and was gone. Julia wept now; tears mingling with the rain pouring down her face and dripping off her nose.

But, as she was about to return to the pavement, she didn't notice the car pulling out from the kerb behind her and gathering speed. Dressed entirely in black, she would have been hard enough for the driver to see, even if he hadn't been dazzled by the bright lights and the rain. In such conditions, he shouldn't have been driving so fast. His car struck her from behind and she rolled across the bonnet before she connected with the windscreen to be tossed in the air to land broken and twisted on the tarmac in front of him. It all happened so quickly, he was almost too shocked to apply the brakes. Beside him, in the passenger seat, his girlfriend started to scream.

Luke, after leaving the hospital by taxi some time later, went to his bachelor pad in town rather than collect his car from the restaurant and drive all the way down the coast. His apartment felt cold and unwelcoming as he hadn't been there for some days and it was only when he opened the fridge that he remembered he had no food. Nor did he feel well enough to go out and buy some. So he passed a restless night, swallowing pain-killers that didn't really work and drinking whisky the hospital doctor had warned him to avoid. The doctor had said he was lucky that, although a bone had been grazed, no major arteries or tendons had been severed. He didn't feel very lucky at all – his hand hurt like hell. So he drank more whisky and fell into a restless sleep around 5 a.m.

Just after 9 a.m. he was roused by the trilling of his mobile. He pulled the covers over his head and tried to ignore it but the caller was insistent, refusing to leave a message.

'Sandford here,' he answered at last, hoping it would be something he could deal with quickly and get back to sleep.

'Oh, Mr Sandford, it's Wendy here. Your new PA.'

'I know that Wendy is my new PA. What do you want?'

'Oh, um—' The girl wilted under his sarcasm. 'It's just— I

had a call as soon as the office was open. From a Ms Canning.'

'Wendy,' he was speaking with exaggerated patience, 'listen carefully because I want you to remember this and pass it on to the rest of the office – I shall be taking no more calls from Ms Julia Canning.'

'No, you don't understand. The call was from a Ms Sarah Canning – Julia's sister. It sounded rather urgent. And you did say I wasn't to give out your mobile number to anyone without checking with you first.'

'I know, I know.' He sighed, controlling his impatience. It wasn't the girl's fault that he found her irritating. 'Give me the number – I'll call her back when I can.'

'No, she insisted that it was urgent and sounded upset,' Wendy persisted. 'But are you OK? You sound like you've got the flu?'

'It's a long story but no, I don't feel the best.'

'Oh dear. I'm sorry.'

'Just give me the number, Wendy.'

He wrote down the number and finally got rid of Wendy who was imploring him to drink honey and hot lemon to soothe a sore throat. What could Julia's sister possibly want? He scarcely remembered meeting her. Surely, she wasn't about to plead with him on her sister's behalf? That didn't sound like Julia at all. She usually fought her own battles. He sighed as he dialled the number, preparing himself for an awkward conversation with a woman he scarcely knew.

'Sarah Canning.' She answered his call, giving him quite a shock. Her voice was so similar to that of her sister.

'How are you, Sarah? Luke Sandford returning your call.'

'Oh, Luke, thank goodness you rang.' The girl's voice cracked and trembled. 'There's no easy way to tell you, but Julia's dead.'

'Dead? No. Someone's having you on. I saw her only last night.'

'That's right. She was killed in the road outside the restaurant. The driver said it was raining and she appeared out of nowhere in front of his car. He said he had no chance of avoiding her.'

Luke's mind whirled; he was having trouble coming to terms with this news. *Julia! Dead!*

'She'd already picked up her wedding dress and was so looking forward to it – to Hawaii. She wanted me to go with her and be her bridesmaid.' Sarah's trembling, grief-stricken voice continued, 'There has to be an inquest so there won't be a funeral right away.' She choked on a sob. 'Talk to the police – I can't tell you any more now.'

'I will,' he said automatically. 'Thanks, Sarah. I'll be in touch later.'

He sat down heavily on the bed. Instead of the relief he expected to feel with Julia gone from his life forever, he felt only remorse and a degree of responsibility for her death. Yes, she had been wilful and selfish, relentless in the pursuit of her own desires, but she had done no real harm to Paige's son. No. Far from being relieved, he felt only guilt that he had handled the matter so badly.

Similar feelings were experienced by Paige and her grand-mother, when Luke dropped by to tell them the news.

'What happened to your hand?' Paige asked, as he came through the back door and she saw his bandaged hand and the sling. 'Don't tell me that Julia—'

'Paige, wait a moment. Let me get a word in edgeways.'

'I'm sorry, Luke, but won't you sit down before you fall down?' She pulled out a chair from the table and he sank into it gratefully. 'You look awful.'

He sat there for several minutes, nursing his head in his free hand. After the night he had passed and the shock that followed it, he needed to collect his thoughts. Shaking her head, Nanou set a cup of coffee in front of him, waiting for him to feel ready to speak. He took a deep breath before raising his head.

'I know this is going to be hard to believe but Julia's dead.'

'How?' Paige said, clapping her hands to her mouth. For one dreadful moment it crossed her mind that Luke might have strangled her. The bandage might be because she had bitten his hand.

Briefly, Luke told them what had happened at the restaurant. Horrified, Paige and Nanou listened as he spoke of his conversations the following morning with both Sarah and the police, telling them all he knew.

'And the case is complicated because the boy's trying to say she ran into the road deliberately. Then his girlfriend let slip to the police that they'd been drinking and the driver wasn't concentrating because they'd been having a row. No doubt the truth will come out at the inquest.'

'Well, I'm sorry for Miss Canning and for her family,' Nanou said at last. 'No one deserves such a shocking, untimely death.'

Paige stared at Luke, understanding only too well what he must be feeling. He looked pale and in need of a good night's sleep. On more than one occasion, she had longed for Julia to be gone from their lives – but no one could have wished it to happen like this.

CHAPTER TEN

Julia's death had driven a wedge between Paige and Luke more certainly than if she had remained alive. In spite of the shared experiences and concern over Marc, an awkwardness had developed between them, making it difficult to find their way back into the easy relationship they had shared before. Somehow the spectre of Julia was always there.

After a verdict of accidental death had been recorded, brushing aside the young driver's attempts to claim suicide, Luke had attended her funeral alone. The church service, which he had hoped would be mercifully brief, turned out to be unusually long, featuring all of Julia's favourite hymns. And, as her sister, Sarah, glanced at him as she came to the end of a long eulogy, Luke felt the first stirring of panic. Until now, she had given him no warning that he might be asked to speak. She spent a good fifteen minutes recalling many incidents from their childhood and praising Julia's virtues before drawing her speech to a close.

'For most of her adult life, Julia was more than a sister to me.' For the first time Sarah showed signs of giving way to her emotions. 'She was the one who kept things going after our mother died.' Once more she glanced towards Luke, her expression less friendly. 'She was always so independent, so strong, I never thought she would marry. No one seemed to measure up to her exacting standards. That is, until she met Luke.' She turned towards him with a tight little smile. 'This must be so hard for you, and I'm sure your heart must be breaking as mine is.' Luke glanced around, wondering if he was the only one aware of the sarcastic meaning of her words. 'But I'm sure you wouldn't want to let Julia pass without adding a few words of your own.' Her eyes glittered as she said this, making her look uncannily like her sister.

Fully aware that Sarah had done this on purpose, wanting to show him up, Luke walked slowly forward to stand before the congregation, collecting his thoughts. 'What more can I possibly say? Sarah has covered everything.' He tried to smile at her but she looked away. 'Julia was' – he hesitated, not wanting to tell an outright lie – 'a woman for whom I had a great respect.' That much had once been true. But even now he found it impossible to say he had loved her although he knew that's what most people expected to hear. 'Julia always had firm goals in her life and set out to achieve them.' He closed his eyes for a moment, unable to banish the image of her vicious expression as he had last seen her, stabbing his hand. 'Her death is a cruel tragedy and she will be sorely missed by both family and friends.' He knew his speech had been lame and hopelessly inadequate but he had no resources left. He couldn't dissemble and pretend he felt more than he did.

As he returned to his seat, he caught sight of Sarah holding back tears and shaking her head.

Afterwards, standing by as the casket was lowered into the ground and aware that everyone would expect him to throw the first handful of earth, he could feel only guilty relief. Later, he felt even worse as people pressed forward to offer whispered condolences – *must be dreadful for you – lovely girl cut down in the prime of life – so sorry for your loss.* Grim-faced and feeling like the worst kind of hypocrite, he allowed the platitudes to wash over him, having nothing to say, the wound in his hand still a throbbing reminder of Julia's obsessive craziness. He was indeed sorry that she should have died so needlessly, but he felt weary and worn down by the day's events. Now all he wanted was to get away.

After the funeral, he paid a short courtesy visit to Sarah's home, noting that there were few relatives of the older generation present, apart from one elderly aunt in a wheelchair who seemed confused and kept asking whose funeral it was. Sarah, alone in the world apart from the man she lived with, had made all the arrangements herself.

Luke tried to leave discreetly as soon as he could, but Sarah wasn't about to let him escape so easily and followed him to his car. Her expression was sombre and he tensed, waiting for the storm to break over his head. Sarah stepped into his space, giving him a searching look.

'I don't know what happened to my sister the night she died. Only that you left her there in the dark and the rain to make her way home alone.'

Wearily, he shook his head. 'It wasn't like that, Sarah,' he said, putting his damaged hand behind his back. He didn't want to tell her the truth and ruin her memory of the perfect sister she had looked up to and adored.

'So how was it then, Luke? I've been watching you all day and you don't look like a man grieving, not to me. I'd say you were guilt personified. I can't help feeling that somehow you are responsible for Julia's death.'

'All right.' He was almost shouting now. 'I do feel responsible but it wasn't my fault—'

'No? I do know you had an affair while you were engaged to her – she told me that much at least. She was very upset.'

'Sarah, believe me, you know only half the tale.'

'Then tell me the rest of it, Luke, because I need to understand.'

He stared at her for a moment, wondering whether to tell her the whole sorry tale. In the end, he decided against it. It would only upset her and she probably wouldn't believe him, anyway. 'Not now, Sarah. This isn't the time. There's been enough sadness today. I am sorry, truly sorry, for what happened to Julia and I do know how inadequate that sounds.'

'And that's it? You think that's enough? Platitudes!' She almost spat the word as tears threatened again. 'You must be as relieved as I am that this is the last time we'll have to see each other. But that's not going to stop me thinking of you all the time and believing the worst of you. Just don't let me hear of you marrying any time soon.' And with that, she turned and stamped back to the house.

Luke drove slowly away, realizing Sarah was right. Although Julia was gone, it left him by no means free to get on with his life. A suitable period of mourning would have to be observed.

Paige reacted differently. She locked away that expensive bottle of perfume, wore no make-up and dressed as plainly as a boy, devoting herself to the work she knew best, riding and training Pierette and Luke's horses. Julia had been buried for more than a month and, in spite of the fact that

159

the spring carnival was now only weeks away, Luke stayed in town, immersing himself in his other business interests. It occurred to her that he was spending more time in the city than he had ever done when Julia was alive. She could only assume that she had been right all along. He had never regarded her as more than a pleasant diversion – as Nanou had so neatly put it – *the sugar and spice in his life*. And now that the woman who had stood so squarely between them was gone, there was no longer a place for her in Luke Sandford's world.

'Why don't you talk to him?' Nanou said at breakfast when Paige returned from the early morning track work looking listless. 'You can't go on like this, punishing one another and feeling guilty. It's ridiculous. That crazy woman has gone and that's no bad thing – in my opinion at least. It's time you put it all behind you and got on with your lives. Why not ask him to lunch on Sunday? Say Marc misses him.'

'He does.' Paige sighed. 'He's always asking when he's going to see Luke again.'

'Then pick up the phone and do it. Or I will.'

'No Nanou, leave it.' Wearily, Paige shook her head. She knew, as her grandmother didn't, the size of the chasm that had opened between them and which seemed to grow wider each day. Those cold little conversations concerning the horses when she could hear an office full of people behind him. No more warm, light-hearted banter or shared intimacy. It was breaking her heart but she couldn't let Nanou see it. She must get on with her life alone.

Having spent so much time with him previously, Paige knew Luke's training methods as well as he did himself. Happy Rosie was gaining strength and looked like being the best of his horses. Texas Joe could no longer be described as an 'old plodder' and they should both do well in the spring carnival. But it was Pierette who was now demonstrating real promise. Having won several major races in the country, she was booked into a race for fillies and mares at Caulfield in mid August. Paige wanted her to be familiar with the track as she hoped she would prove to be a contender for the Caulfield Cup in October. She was to ride Texas Joe for Luke on the same day. As yet she didn't dare even to dream that Pierette might qualify for the big race in November.

Although it was winter in Melbourne, the weather was mild. It had been very cold the night before, heralding fine weather for the following day. Gail and Glenda set off early with the two horses in the float. Pierette and Texas Joe had been noticed by the bookmakers and both were well favoured to win.

After seeing them off, Paige realized she didn't feel much like breakfast and the thought of coffee that normally she craved, disgusted her. Used to being in rude health and on top of her form, she was surprised to feel so unwell – nauseous even. She scarcely reached the toilet at the stables before she vomited. It was Ham Peachey who heard her and came to see what was wrong.

'If you'm sick, you shouldn't be riding today. Want me to ring Mr Sandford and say so?'

'No, Ham. It must be something I ate and it's gone now. I'll be OK.'

'Eh, well. Not Superwoman, are ye? For all ye'd have us believe. Push yoursel' too hard, you do. Sommat's gotta give.'

This was the nearest thing to a compliment she had ever received from Ham and it made her smile. But she was feeling better now and ready to cope with the day ahead.

After driving to the course, she realized her energy levels were low and she didn't feel quite so well as she thought. Impatiently, she brushed the feeling aside, not wanting to give up her rides to a substitute jockey. She knew Taffy Evans regretted what happened before and was always watching and waiting, anxious to regain his position with Luke.

Texas Joe's race was early on in the day. To Paige's relief, he did exactly as was expected. With only a small field against him, he took up the leading position as soon as they were out of the gates and never looked as if he would lose it. He won comfortably, five lengths in front of the rest of the field. Now aware of the horse's foibles, Paige sat tight, giving him no opportunity to tip her off. She returned to the winner's position and dismounted to a rousing cheer from the crowd. Everyone loved a favourite who could win; most people had backed him and made money.

Suddenly nauseous again, Paige fled to the changing rooms with scarcely a word to Luke who was trying to thank her.

'You should call it a day.' One of the other girls came and stood in the door to the bathroom, watching her splash water on her burning face. 'No fun riding when you have a stomach upset – I've done it myself.'

'Only one more ride today.' Paige croaked. 'I'll be OK.'

'Well, I hope so.' The girl folded her arms. 'You'll put everyone else at risk if you pass out on the horse and fall off.'

'I told you. I'm OK,' Paige snapped.

Outside again, she sat down on a bench, feeling shaky. Was it possible? Was she really likely to pass out and fall, endangering everyone else?

The other girl followed her out, bringing a glass of iced

water. 'I could ride for you if you don't feel up to it?' she said tentatively. 'I ride very light.'

Paige smiled. So that's what this was about. This girl didn't think she was sick enough to fall off— she was trying to poach the ride.

'Cheers!' Paige raised the glass of water and took a larger gulp than she wanted, to prove the point. 'I told you, I'm fine now. And Pierette is my grandmother's horse – I don't want to give up the ride.'

The girl shrugged and walked away.

But she wasn't the only person to remark on her pallor. Gail looked at her in concern when she was holding Pierette steady, waiting for Paige to mount.

'You look like death warmed up – are you feeling OK?'

'I was until you mentioned it,' Paige quipped. 'Very encouraging.'

'I'm sorry, Paige, but you're white as a sheet. Should you be—'

'How many more times?' Paige snatched the reins from Gail, turning Pierette away as she encouraged her into a trot. 'I'm OK.'

As they walked the horses around, waiting to go into the starting gates, Paige seriously began to wonder if that other jockey and Gail had been right. Having voided her stomach completely, she was feeling a little dizzy and light-headed. Too late now. She must do the best she could.

There were quite a few fillies and mares in this race – a much larger field than before – and having been immersed in her own gloomy thoughts, Paige almost missed the start. As the field galloped ahead of her, she had to be content to take up a far from ideal position at the rear, hoping for an opportunity to overtake them at the finish. Fortunately, Pierette knew her business as Paige was beyond strategy;

hanging on doggedly, just hoping to finish the race in one piece.

But as they rounded the home turn and the field spread out across the track, Pierette showed her class, seizing the opportunity to come through, overtaking them all. Paige, who had been riding by instinct, trying not to pass out, could take no credit for the fact that they won. Pierette had done it all by herself.

Later, when she had returned the horse to Gail, weighed in and changed, she set off for home, as far as possible avoiding the motorways; she didn't feel up to that kind of aggressive driving. Her empty stomach rumbled, reminding her that she'd had nothing to eat all day. Thinking she was starving, she stopped for a break at Macdonald's but as soon as she entered the café, the smell of sizzling burgers made her feel sick all over again. She left quickly. Nanou would be sure to have something ready when she got home – good, wholesome home-cooking, that's what she needed. On the way, she considered this sickness, wondering when she had felt like this before and whether she should make one of her rare visits to her doctor. When the answer came to her, she nearly ran off the road.

The drive took her longer than usual and she arrived home well after dark to find Nanou waiting anxiously in the kitchen and Marc already in bed.

'Great heavens, Paige, what kept you?' she said. 'I don't like to call you when you're out on the road but Gail and Glenda came home with the float hours ago. I was afraid you'd had an accident.'

'And you'd be right. An accident is exactly what I've had. I think I'm pregnant, Nanou.'

'Oh, that's nice.' The old lady didn't miss a beat. 'A baby brother or sister for Marc.'

'It's not nice at all. It's horribly inconvenient. And, what's more, I don't know how it happened.'

'Ah well, *chérie*, you go to bed with a man and you—'

'Don't tease me, I can't bear it. The only man I've slept with is Luke and he told me he's had a vasectomy.'

'And you believed him?' Nanou gave a short bark of laughter.

'This isn't funny, Nanou. I wish you'd treat it more seriously. Why should Luke lie to me? He has as much to lose from an unwanted pregnancy as I do.'

'Think about it, *chérie*. This isn't a tragedy. It may be just what is needed to bring you and Luke together again.'

'Or drive us further apart. I could kill him for this; for deceiving me. If I have another baby, it's the end of my riding career. And what are we going to live on, apart from anything else?'

'Something always turns up.' Nanou shrugged. 'You'll get your trainer's licence and take it from there.'

'Between Sunny Orchards and ourselves, we already have three trainers with licences around here.'

'Well, I'm happy to stand aside for you. That's what I planned on doing eventually – I don't mind if it has to be now. And, as for the riding – pouff! – that isn't important. There are always talented new apprentices coming up.'

'But *I* wanted to ride. For a few more years at least. I've got an agent interested in me now and I'm getting a good reputation after those city wins.'

'Listen to yourself. How can you stress on such trivial matters?'

'Trivial?' Paige said, through gritted teeth. 'Not to me. Can't you see that this is a recipe for financial disaster?'

Nanou smiled. 'A child is a blessing, Paige – a gift from God.'

'Or from a lying bastard who pretended to be infertile when he's not.'

Nanou shrugged. 'Look at it however you like. And whether it makes you 'appy or sad, this baby is coming and Luke will 'ave to be told.'

'I've a good mind to get rid of it and say nothing to anyone.'

'Now you know you don't mean that.'

Paige shrugged, wanting to shake Nanou from her smug acceptance of the situation. 'It depends how desperate I get.'

'Go and see Doctor Hazell first. You could be worrying about nothing and might not be pregnant at all.'

'I wish.'

Nanou shook her head, rolling her eyes heavenwards.

Paige liked June Hazell who was a family doctor as well as an obstetrician; a young woman just a few years older than herself. Around the time Marc was born, Paige had needed a lot of support and they had become firm friends. After spending about ten minutes giggling and catching up – both of them had children of similar age – June glanced at her watch.

'Better cut to the chase, Paige. What brings you here? You're usually in such rude health? Marc OK?'

'Marc's fine. I'm here about me.' Paige sighed. 'I might have got myself pregnant.'

'And from the sound of it, you're not pleased.' The doctor consulted her computer, looking up Paige's notes. 'We don't have you on the pill, do we?'

'There was no need. I've been home with Nanou and living like a nun since Ruary died.'

'But not any more. Are you sure about this? Have you

166

done any tests for yourself?'

'No. But the signs are all there. I have morning sickness and my breasts are sore. And I know exactly when it happened.'

'So there's no doubt who the father is?'

'None at all.' Paige scowled. 'And I could cheerfully murder him for getting me into this.'

June's expression clouded. 'You seem to harbour a lot of resentment towards him which isn't good for you or the baby. And it takes two to tango, you know. You have to accept some responsibility for this.'

'I don't think so. Not when he told me he'd had a vasectomy.'

'Ah. If I had a dollar for every time I've heard that one, I'd be a rich woman. OK. Hop up on the couch and let's take a look.'

It didn't take long for June to confirm what Paige already knew. She had been pregnant for the best part of three months.

'And if—' Paige was suddenly tentative and spoke in a low voice. This wasn't something she had discussed with her doctor before. 'If I wanted to get rid of it?'

'Now surely that's only a last resort?'

'June, if I have this baby, it's going to change my whole life.'

'Babies usually do.' The doctor smiled. 'I'm an obstetrician – not in the business of terminations myself. Why not talk to the father about it first. See if you can't work something out.'

'I don't expect him to marry me, if that's what you mean. I've never been anything more to him than a workmate, a mistress at best.'

'So he's married already?'

'No, it's not that. He had a fiancée but she died.' Paige looked away. She didn't feel like discussing what happened to Julia.

'Ah, so you're both on the guilt trip.' June sat back, studying her patient, her head on one side. 'I think you could do with some counselling – of the professional kind. You never had any after Ruary died.'

'I didn't need it then and I don't need it now.' Suddenly furious, Paige sprang to her feet, grabbing her jacket and getting ready to leave. 'You think I'm crazy just because I don't want a baby at this time in my life.'

'Paige, sit down. That's a knee-jerk reaction and it's stupid. Counselling is for anyone who needs it, not just crazy people. But first I think you'd better tell me the whole story – not just the sanitized version for good old Doc Hazell – then we can decide what is best to do.'

Half an hour and half a box of tissues later, June knew everything. Her receptionist had knocked on the door ten minutes ago, reminding the doctor that she had a roomful of people out there, only to be sent away with a flea in her ear.

'I'm sorry,' Paige sobbed. 'I didn't mean to be such a nuisance.'

'It's OK. All of my patients are important to me.' June took her hand. 'And if those people out there don't like waiting, they should remember that without watching the clock I give each and every one of them as much care and attention as they need.'

Eventually, Paige left, promising not to do anything drastic until she had discussed the situation with Luke. Oddly enough, she had the greatest difficulty in deciding where to meet him. Although she still saw him regularly for work at Sunny Orchards, there were always too many people around to have a private discussion. And, if she asked him to come to *Warrender*, Marc wouldn't give them five minutes alone. It was Nanou who found the solution.

'There's a new *Shrek* film at the local cinema and you know how Marc loves them. We'll go to an early afternoon session and have popcorn, so you can have the house to yourselves. That should allow more than two hours for you to give him your news. I'll leave you some lasagna so you don't have to cook.'

'Good. Because Luke may not feel much like eating when I've finished with him. We can have it for supper when you and Marc come home.'

Nanou studied her granddaughter, biting her lip. 'I'm not sure that this is a good idea. Perhaps you should wait another week or so until you've got used to it and calmed down.'

'I'm not going to get used to it and I certainly won't calm down. I want to leave him in no doubt of the mess he has made of my life.'

Nanou sighed. 'Think about it, Paige. You didn't have to sleep with him, did you? You can't lay all the blame at Luke's door.'

'Funny. That's exactly what June Hazell said.'

'And she was right.'

Luke seemed exceptionally pleased to receive her invitation to lunch, accepting quickly as if he thought she might change her mind.

'It will be so good to talk, really talk to each other and catch up,' he said. And then hesitantly, 'Paige does this mean—?'

'It means nothing more than I'm inviting you here for lunch,' she snapped back, although her heart betrayed her at the sound of that particular timbre in his voice, setting up a painful rhythm, making it hard for her to get her breath. She had forgotten how susceptible she was; how easily he could charm and seduce her. Deliberately, she took a deep breath to calm herself, refusing to let her feelings get the better of her. 'Please be here some time before one.'

'Look forward to seeing you – and Marc. It's been too long.'

Paige terminated the call, not trusting herself to say anything more.

Although she knew they would both feel more comfortable having a meal together before the stove in the old farmhouse kitchen, Paige made a setting for two at one end of the table in the formal dining-room. There was a chill in the air as the room was seldom used so she brought in an electric heater to warm it, not wanting to offer the welcome of an open fire. Nanou's lasagna was already cooked and needed only reheating. Thoughtfully, the old lady had provided a green salad to go with it and it sat there looking crisp and appetizing in a vintage crystal bowl with servers to match. Nanou had also suggested candles but Paige wouldn't hear of it.

At midday, she told Nanou to stop fussing and go. If Luke should arrive early and Marc saw him, not even the prospect of *Shrek* would tempt him away.

It was as well that she sent them off early because Luke arrived soon after 12.30. He brought her a large bunch of expensive liliums which she scarcely acknowledged, placing them in the kitchen sink and filling it with water to revive them. Nanou could find a vase for them later on. He also brought some white wine to go with the meal as well as two bottles of Moët for Nanou.

'So they're not here,' he said, surprised to find Paige alone and quick to pick up on her less-than-welcoming attitude. 'Just the two of us, then?'

'Just us,' she said with a thin smile.

'Now why do I get the feeling this isn't good news?'

Paige herself had been taken by surprise. She had spent so much time being angry with Luke and rehearsing all the harsh words she would say to him, she had forgotten entirely the pull of attraction he always had for her, the way he could fill a room with his presence, becoming instantly at ease anywhere.

'Sit down,' she said in a voice that wasn't as steady as she would have liked. 'There's something I have to tell you and something to ask.'

'Get on with it then.' He did as she asked, folding his arms and looking at her expectantly. 'Let's get the bad stuff out of the way so we can enjoy ourselves.'

'Oh, I wish it were that simple, Luke. This isn't something that will easily go away.'

'Let's open the wine, then. It's already chilled. I can cope with a dressing down better with a glass in my hand.'

'Go ahead. But nothing for me. I'm not drinking at present.' Paige watched as he expertly opened the bottle and poured himself a generous glass.

'Fire away,' he said. 'What am I supposed to have done now?'

'This time it's something you *haven't* done. Do you remember in the dim and distant past of some three months ago, you told me you'd had a vasectomy?'

'Ohh?' he said slowly.

'Oh, indeed. How could you be so irresponsible? One night maybe I could forgive. You could say we were carried away in the moment. But you made unprotected love to me

171

over that whole weekend. And told me a bare-faced lie.'

'Now, wait. Wait just a moment – I can explain.'

'I'm listening. And it had better be good. Because I'm *enceinte*! Knocked up! To put it even more plainly – I have a bun in the oven.'

To her fury, he smiled. 'Well don't expect me to regard it as such bad news.'

'It's terrible news.' She was becoming shrill. 'You're an idiot! Just like Nanou!'

'So she agrees with me. That's why you've sent her out.'

'You're not hearing me. Don't you realize what this means? I won't be able to ride in the spring carnival – I may never ride professionally again. But we're getting ahead of ourselves. I'm still waiting to hear your explanation for lying to me.'

'OK. Let's back up a moment here. I could see you were desperately worried that night and you needed me to say something reassuring. It didn't seem such a great big lie at the time. My wife took two years to fall pregnant with Alan and never stopped complaining that she thought the deficiency was all mine.'

'Yes, but you went much further than that. You told me that after Alan was born, your wife wouldn't sleep with you until you'd had a vasectomy.'

'Well, yeah.' He had the grace to look sheepish. 'That was maybe a little creative.'

'A *little*!'

'Paige, it was our first night together – we weren't even in a relationship. I didn't know if you wanted one long term – it was all so new.'

'And that's your excuse for deceiving me? Everything you say now is just making it worse.'

'Honestly, Paige, I thought we were safe. I didn't think I

was that fertile. It never occurred to me that it might be different with you.'

'You didn't stop to think about anything, Luke. And now here I am inconveniently pregnant.'

'I know and I think it's wonderful. I want to shout it from the roof-tops.' He still didn't seem to register that she was really upset. 'We have to be practical now. When are we going to—?'

'Don't go hanging the flags out just yet.' She cut him off quickly before he could say anything more. 'I haven't decided whether I'm keeping it.' She was satisfied to see the smile wiped instantly off his face as if she had slapped him. 'After all, it's my body. My choice.'

'Paige, don't. Don't even joke about making such a choice.'

'I'm not joking. Why should I consider your feelings? Not for one moment have you considered mine.'

He stared at her for a long moment before standing up. 'I can't do this,' He said. 'Not now. And not after all we've been through. I can't sit here and calmly eat lunch while you talk so casually about destroying our child.'

'It's no worse than you casually destroying my life.'

'Paige, enough now.' He couldn't bring himself to look at her as he headed for the door. 'Give my love to Marc and Nanou – say I'm sorry I missed them. I'll talk to you when you're in a better frame of mind.'

As soon as she saw that he meant what he said and really was leaving, Paige had a change of heart. She would have stopped him and said she was sorry, but it was too late. A few long strides took him through the back door as she ran after him, wondering what on earth to say. She was certain he knew she was watching him as he opened the car and got in but not once did he glance in her direction before driving away. After he'd gone, Paige burst into tears. How could she have been such a fool? She couldn't understand her own feelings now. How was it possible to feel so angry with him and yet love him so much? She was still crying when Marc and Nanou came home.

CHAPTER ELEVEN

Stubborn to a fault and despite Doctor Hazell's warnings, Paige ignored her condition and kept riding professionally. She also refused the counselling that the doctor hoped she would take. True to his word, Luke stayed away although he knew what was happening at *Warrender* on a daily basis, keeping in touch via discreet telephone conversations with Nanou.

'She's not going to give in, Luke,' Nanou sighed. 'Even her doctor is worried about her now. She tried to shock some sense into Paige by telling her if she continues to be so irresponsible, she could miscarry the child. Sometimes I wonder if that's what she's trying to do. If she were to lose it naturally, no blame will attach to her.'

'Surely she doesn't want that?' Luke groaned. 'She doesn't hate me that much, does she?'

'I don't think she hates you at all. That's what the problem is.'

'Then why won't she talk to me? Let me help sort things out?'

'She is confused. Some women go right off the planet during pregnancy and I'm afraid Paige is one of them. You should've seen her when she was carrying Marc. At the time I thought it was due to bereavement but now I'm not so sure. On top of that, she has a new maggot in her head.'

'Oh, God. What now?'

'She's saying you must have known she was fertile because she has Marc. You got her pregnant deliberately because you wanted a child to replace your son. Did you ever hear such a crazy notion?'

'No. But she can't go on like this, Nanou. One way or another, she's going to make herself ill.'

'I know. I know.' The old lady started, hearing a door bang and Marc's little footsteps running in the hall. 'I 'ave to go now. Paige and Marc have come home.'

'Right. But call me again when you can.'

Paige came into the kitchen, carrying Marc's satchel, the little boy running ahead of her, anxious to tell Nanou about his day.

'Who were you talking to?' she said to Nanou, who was guiltily snapping her cell phone shut.

'No one important.' The old lady waved the question away as she gave her attention to pouring a glass of milk for Marc and watching him drink it greedily.

Paige smiled ruefully. 'You're a terrible liar, Nanou. It was Luke, wasn't it?'

'What if it was? He's worried about you. We both are.'

'Then he can stop it right now. Because I'm OK. And the next time he calls you can tell him to mind his own business.'

'Is Luke coming to see us?' Marc'c face lit up with expectation.

'No, he's not,' Paige snapped at him. 'Wipe that milk off your mouth and you can go and see Gail and Glenda at the stables.'

'I don't want to.' The little boy pouted, unusually stubborn. 'I want to see Luke.'

'Too bad. We can't always have what we want, Marc.'

Nanou watched the exchange, but said nothing until Marc had gone, carefully carrying a plate of sandwiches to share with Glenda and Gail.

'I know that you're tired and not feeling well, Paige—'

'I'm fine.'

'You may be fine but Marc certainly isn't. You find fault and snap at him all the time. It's not fair to take your temper and your misery out on him.'

'I don't want him depending on a deceitful man like Luke. You can go on championing the man and leasing him space at the stables – that's your business. And I'll go on riding track work for him because we need the money. But on a personal level he's no longer a part of my life.'

'He will always be a part of your life if you share a child.'

Paige groaned. 'Oh, please. Don't bring up that old argument again. Can't we talk about something else? Pierette was terrific at track work today. I'm really looking forward to taking her round in the Caulfield Cup.'

Nanou's eyes widened in dismay. 'But that's not till October – you'll be over twenty weeks and the child will be starting to show—'

'I can count. And I wish everyone would stop building castles in the air. There may not even *be* a baby by then.'

'I don't like it when you talk that way. You're playing a very dangerous game, Paige. I know you think you hold all the cards, but Luke will never forgive you if you deliberately lose this child.'

Paige burst into noisy tears. 'All I hear from you is how I should consider the feelings of Luke and Marc,' she managed to say between sobs. 'Don't you care about me any more?'

Nanou gathered her in to comfort her as if she were a child. 'Hush, *chérie*. Of course I care about you most of all – 'ave I not been mother, father and grandma to you over all these years?'

'I just want this one season – just one spring carnival. Is that so much to ask?'

Nanou sighed. 'I don't know. Talk to Doctor Hazell about it. Maybe you can do it if she says it's OK. But promise me you'll abide by her decision.'

'You're fine and everything's progressing as it should,' June Hazell pronounced after giving Paige a thorough examination.

'So, if I'm fine and the baby's well, there's no reason why I can't keep on riding professionally, is there?'

'Now don't put words into my mouth.' June's smile faded. 'I didn't say that. You don't have to give up riding completely – not yet. But I don't think it would be wise for you to take part in the competitive business of racing. And certainly not at over twenty weeks when the baby is growing so quickly. You'll be putting on weight and starting to show. And besides, I don't want you starving yourself to keep your weight down – that wouldn't be good for you or the child.'

'So what can I do?'

June smiled. 'Give in to the inevitable. Resign yourself to being a mum this year. Maybe next year you can—'

'But you don't understand,' Paige wailed. 'If I have to stop now, I'll never get back to this level of fitness again. Never—'

'Never isn't always as final as it sounds. You'd be surprised what you can achieve if you want it enough.'

Paige left the doctor's office feeling as though she'd

backed herself into a corner. She had been feeling much better since the morning sickness had abated and had been so sure June Hazell would support her in what she wanted to do. For the time being, she decided not to say anything to Nanou. All the same, she started training Glenda to ride Pierette. The mare was already qualified to run in the Caulfield Cup and was used to a girl on her back. Gail didn't have quite the same flair and ability, but Glenda seemed more than capable of taking the ride. Inevitably, she knew she must confide in the twins and tell them why she wouldn't be riding Pierette herself. She approached the two girls before track work at Sunny Orchards.

'I'd love to ride Pierette in a major race – of course I would.' Glenda's eyes sparkled at the thought. 'But you've always taken her round yourself. This should be your year, Paige – you've already won the Golden Slipper on Rosie and Pierette looks all set for the Caulfield Cup. Why are you backing off now?'

'Because,' Paige hesitated, giving a rueful smile. 'My doctor advises against it.'

'Why? You're not sick, are you?' Gail asked. 'You don't look sick to me. You're almost glowing. I'd even say you've put on some weight around your face.'

'That's exactly it.' Paige smiled at them. 'And by the time the Caulfield Cup comes around, I'll be putting on a lot more. I'm expecting a baby—'

'A baby!' Glenda almost shrieked.

'Hush!' Paige said, glancing anxiously around to see if anyone else had heard. The stable at Sunny Orchards was a hotbed of gossip. 'It's not common knowledge yet.'

'A baby!' Gail repeated in a hushed whisper. 'I didn't even know you had a boyfriend.'

'I don't.'

179

'Ooh.' Gail looked thoughtful. 'So how did it happen? Did the Angel Gabriel come down and tell you—'

'Don't be daft, Sis,' Glenda broke in on the joke, giving her twin a friendly push. 'You know. She'll have done it with a turkey baster and somebody's—?'

'Ew!' Said Gail, making Paige laugh.

'No – I know.' Glenda nodded sagely. 'It happened while we were in Sydney, didn't it? You had loads of opportunity and I thought I spotted a funny-looking mark on your neck.' She jerked her head towards Luke who was looking through a pair of binoculars watching horses going round on the training track. 'And then taking that leisurely drive back home with himself. It all fits. Have you told him yet?'

'I've told the two of you just as much as you need to know,' Paige said. 'And I'd be grateful if you keep it to yourselves – for now. It will be obvious to everyone else soon enough.'

'And has he asked you to marry him?' Gail had never been known for her tact. 'Now that awful woman has gone?' Paige had already told them that Julia was responsible for Marc's disappearance that day.

'I've hardly seen him lately.' Paige sighed. 'But that's not really his fault. It's mine.' She clapped her hands, changing the subject. 'Come on. Time's a-wasting and we've got horses to exercise.' She got Gail to give her a leg up into Texas Joe's saddle.

She trotted him out on to the training track, Glenda taking another horse to compete with him and make him try harder. Gail was to time their run with a stop watch.

Texas Joe gave his all, working his way round the track to beat the other horse easily by several lengths and he pulled up, blowing hard. Absentmindedly, Paige walked him to let him cool down and patted his neck to praise him for his effort. But, as they turned to trot back to Gail who was grinning and holding her thumb up, indicating he had made good time, something caught the light to the left of his field of vision and spooked him. Without warning he reared and bucked, taking Paige by surprise and tossing her out of the saddle. Instinctively, as she fell she cradled her belly to protect the baby but this didn't stop her from landing awkwardly, jarring her spine on ground that was still winter-hard.

Glenda rode off to recapture the horse while everyone else came running to help Paige, including Luke, who had been watching the performance of Texas Joe. Gingerly, she allowed him to help her to her feet and support her, believing in those first few moments that no harm had been done. She began to breathe again, thinking she might have got away with it, after all.

'It's all right,' she whispered, meeting Luke's anxious gaze. 'I'm OK.'

'All the same, you're getting a check-up.' He snapped his fingers, asking for her mobile. 'Give me your doctor's number.'

Predictably, June Hazell's receptionist told him the list for that morning was full and June had no vacancies even for an emergency that day.

'If Mrs McHugh's had an accident, you should go to the hospital.' The woman was pleasant but firm. 'We aren't an emergency service here.'

'Bollocks!' Luke said, making the woman gasp. 'She needs to see Doctor Hazell and I'm bringing her in right away.'

On the way to June's surgery, Paige discovered that she wasn't at all OK. A dull pain had started up in the base of her spine – the sort of pain that made her wonder if some harm had been done after all and her sides ached, making her think she might be about to bleed. She didn't complain when Luke broke all the speed limits to get to the doctor's surgery in record time.

Wrapped in his car rug because she was white with the shock and pain of what was happening, she didn't protest when he swung her into his arms and carried her inside.

As luck would have it, June was between appointments and in the reception area. Quick to assess the situation, she motioned Luke to carry Paige into her surgery. Even then, the receptionist tried to block them.

'Really, Doctor Hazell,' she said. 'You already have a full list. I told them to go to the hospital. We don't have the facilities for—'

'Thank you, Elise.' Doctor Hazell cut her objections short. 'I know you like things to run smoothly here and on time. But I'll be the one to decide what we can and can't do.' She smiled reassuringly at Luke as he deposited Paige on the couch in the surgery. 'Do you mind waiting outside now? I'll let you know what's happening to Paige as soon as I know myself.'

'Thanks.' Luke, only too happy to be dismissed, took a seat as far away from the eagle-eyed receptionist as he could. He sat there, feeling helpless, flicking through a magazine and seeing nothing. In the end, he sat there for a good half-hour, wondering how he would feel if Paige miscarried their child.

Eventually, June Hazell opened the door and summoned him.

'Paige tells me you are the baby's father,' she said, inviting him to take a seat. Paige was still lying down on the couch. 'And there's no need to look so anxious because the news isn't all bad. She's a bit bruised from the fall but she isn't bleeding, so I'm hoping that we've got away with it. I'll

give you a note for her to get a scan to make quite sure –
there may be bleeding near the placenta that we can't see.
If the scan checks out OK, bed rest for a couple of days
ought to complete the healing process.'

'Thank you, Doctor,' he said, glancing at Paige to see how
she was taking this news. She looked small, vulnerable and
he found her expression impossible to read.

'I want you to take this as a serious warning,' June said,
including both of them in what she was saying.
'Fortunately, Paige is a strong, healthy girl and this time it
looks as if you've had a lucky escape. If there's a next time
– and let's hope there isn't – you may not be so fortunate.'

In spite of Paige's protests that she wanted to walk, Luke
carried her back to his car and ordered her to lie down on
the back seat. At the hospital, he insisted on finding a
wheelchair. After more than a few anxious moments, the
scan confirmed Doctor Hazell's opinion that the placenta
remained intact and the foetus was unharmed.

Before driving back to *Warrender*, he telephoned Nanou,
quickly telling her about the scare and asking her to have
a warm bed waiting for Paige.

'Luke, I'm not sick,' she protested weakly, still lying on
the back seat of his car.

'Well, just for once, pretend that you are,' he snapped
back at her. 'If I could have this baby for you, I would. But
I'm not built that way. All I can do is sit on the sidelines
and watch, hoping you don't mess up.'

'You'd keep me chained to my bed for the whole nine
months if you could.'

'Yes! Yes, I would.' His temper flared. 'If you're trying to
lose this baby on purpose, you're not doing so badly at all.
Why not go riding tomorrow and finish the job?'

'Luke!'

'What? Having seen how you've put us through hell with your pig-headed determination to ride, I was hoping that you'd see reason and take some notice of what Doctor Hazell said. Fat chance.' He heard her gasp but he kept his eyes on the road and didn't look round. 'And it's not just this baby you'll lose, you know. If that happens, you might not be able to have any more.' He waited for that remark to sink in. 'Oh, but how stupid of me. Maybe that's what you want. Then you can go on riding professionally until you're a shrivelled old prune of a female jockey at fifty.'

Having said all that, he waited for her to rise to the bait and let fly at him in return but she didn't A glance in the rear-view mirror showed him that she was sitting up, crying quietly into her hands, tears dripping from between her fingers.

Immediately contrite, he pulled over on the hard shoulder and stopped, opening the back door to crouch beside her.

'Oh God, Paige, I'm so sorry. I'm a beast. I shouldn't be saying such things to you now.'

'No, you shouldn't.' She removed her hands to look at him through red-rimmed eyes, tears still dripping off her lashes. 'Not that I don't deserve it – all of it. I have been pig-headed and stupid. And I'm so tired; I've been nasty to Marc as well.'

'I've been so scared for you. And so afraid you weren't taking care of yourself.'

'I don't have any choice now, do I?' She pulled out an inadequate tissue and blew her nose. 'It was only when I thought I might lose our baby, that I realized how much I wanted him.'

'Or her.'

184

'You won't be disappointed if it isn't a boy?'

'Of course not. In some ways it might be easier. Marc is less likely to feel jealous of a baby girl. Oh, Paige, I don't know what came over me. Can you forgive me for what I said?'

'I must have put you through worse. But Luke you don't have to feel responsible for me. I don't expect—'

'We don't have to talk about this now. Lie down and try to relax while I get you home.'

As soon as Luke lifted Paige from the car, Nanou opened the front door and came running to meet them, Marc at her heels. Luke smiled, hoping to reassure him.

'What's happened to Mummy?' The little boy was quick to notice her pallor as she lay resting in Luke's arms. 'Is she sick?'

'No, mate, she'll be right as ninepence in a day or so,' Luke reassured him. 'Had a little accident over at my place and just needs to rest in bed. She'll be OK soon.'

Carrying Paige as easily as if she weighed nothing at all, he took her upstairs and deposited her in her bed. 'And don't you move from there,' he warned her, 'until Doctor Hazell says.'

Paige sighed. 'All right. But I'm going to get awfully bored, lying in bed.'

'Then I'll get you a television for your room. Marc can come with me to choose it. You already have cable here, don't you?'

'Not upstairs.'

'That's easily fixed. I know some of the guys at Foxtel.'

She smiled. 'Pulling strings again? Is there nobody influential that you don't know?'

He considered this for a moment. 'Not in this town. No.'

185

Downstairs, while Paige lay in bed, having fallen into an exhausted sleep, Nanou thrust a glass of Bushmills into Luke's hand.

'Get that down you,' she ordered. 'You look as if you need it.'

'Thanks.' He sat down at the table and swallowed it gratefully although he knew it was a bribe. Nanou would want information in return for her hospitality.

'So.' The old lady sat opposite him, resting her chin on her hands and regarding him. 'How do things stand now between you and Paige?'

He thought about this for a moment. 'I'm not sure. I said some terrible things to her on the way home, but, somehow, that was the catalyst for clearing the air. She's stopped being angry about the baby and even admitted she wants it – which is progress, I suppose. But how we shall go on from here, I don't really know.'

Nanou shook her head. 'Sometimes she's her own worst enemy. Has no idea how to handle men.'

'I'm not sure I want to be *handled*.' Luke pulled a wry face. 'I've always found her honesty more refreshing.'

'Well, I promise you, she 'as no shortage of that.'

In record time, a plasma television was fixed to the wall in Paige's bedroom, at an angle where she could watch it while lying in bed. Because Marc had a hand in choosing it, the frame surrounding the screen was a lurid pink as he insisted on that and no other. Excited, the little boy bounced on the bed until Luke gently reminded him to stop. 'If you're sitting on your mum's bed, you have to be still,' he said. 'She needs peace and quiet.' Immediately, Marc complied, making Paige smile. A boisterous, healthy child, he wasn't always so obedient.

186

'This is an invitation to laziness, you know,' she teased, as she flicked through the channels until she found a cartoon channel and Marc asked her to stop. Instantly he was absorbed, mouth agape and eyes wide as he watched a superhero swing from a high building to rescue a screaming girl. 'With all that entertainment at the touch of a button, I may never get up at all. I'll just lie in bed, eating and growing fatter and fatter until I look like Jabba The Hut.'

For just a moment, Luke's smile faltered until Paige laughed. 'Do you always have to take me so literally?' she said. 'You should see your face.'

'Paige, we need to make plans.' Ignoring her frivolity, he was suddenly serious. 'What do you think about getting married before the baby is born?' He was surprised to see her expression change, looking less than pleased. 'What now? I'd have thought that's what you'd want, but, as usual, I'm wrong.'

'Why do we have to marry just to keep things right, tight and conventional? I don't need that, Luke. I told you already I expect nothing more.'

'But have you thought that maybe *I* do? I need to be really connected to you – partners for life.'

'Hmm.' She considered this for a moment. 'Is it really me that you want, or a connection to this baby? In all the time that I've known you, you've never told me you love me. Not once.'

He stared at her, disbelieving. 'What? After all that we've been through, you want swooping violins? Hearts and flowers as well? Haven't I shown you how much I love you a thousand times? Do you really need me to spell it out? If it hadn't been for Julia, I would have—'

'Stop it right there,' she said. 'Don't make her your

excuse. You can't hide behind Julia. Not any more.'

'I'm not. God give me patience.' He stood up and starting pacing the room and scrubbing his fingers through his hair. 'I never met a woman so infuriating – so capable of turning everything inside out as you do.'

'*I'm* infuriating? This is playing out like a scene from *The Taming of the Shrew.*'

'Isn't it though.'

'Luke, you just offered me marriage, yet here you are, bawling me out before I've had time to consider it.'

'You're not considering anything, you're turning me down.'

Hearing their raised voices, Marc was momentarily distracted from his cartoon.

'You're not fighting with Luke again, are you?' he said to his mother. 'I don't like that. Because he'll go away again and I shan't see him for ages like last time.'

Paige took a deep breath and smiled at both of them, trying to relax.

'*Pas devant,*' she muttered, rolling her eyes towards Marc, whose attention had been reclaimed by the television. 'We need to settle this later, when we're alone.'

But in spite of Nanou and Luke's almost constant urging – or maybe because of it – Paige had still not made a firm promise to marry him. Slender as she was, in this fifth month of her pregnancy she was just starting to show.

'What are you waiting for, *chérie?*' Nanou pleaded with her yet again, when she came in from supervising track work, her mind buzzing with her plans for Pierette and Glenda in the spring carnival rather than a spring wedding. 'The man's ready and willing so why do you 'esitate? He has his pride too, you know, and might not wait forever.'

'Then I'll know it was not meant to be.' Paige was stubborn in her philosophy.

'I don't understand you. I was so sure you were deeply in love with him.'

'Well, of course I am, but—'

'But what? Luke adores you and Marc thinks the world of him, so what is stopping you from taking that final step?'

'Give it a rest, Nanou. I'm not getting married now until the baby is here and I can have a proper "day out". Right now, this isn't the time. I have to keep my mind on Pierette. The Caulfield Cup is going to be her greatest challenge and I have to make sure that she's ready. Glenda, too. I have to build up her confidence.'

'Are you sure she's up to it? She's only just started her apprenticeship really, and to ride for us in such an important race—'

'Pierette is responding to her as well as she does to me. All Glenda has to do is keep focused and conquer her nerves.'

'An' that may be easier said that done. Remember how you were when you started.'

'This isn't like you, Nanou. You're usually so supportive of those girls.'

'I am. I love both of them. But I wonder if you are promoting Glenda past her ability.'

'Too late now. The race is on Saturday and she has the ride.'

But although Paige was still dragging her feet about marriage, this didn't prevent her from inviting Luke to go with her to see the ultrasound scan. At twenty weeks this was an important one. Not only would it determine if all was well but it would also show them the sex of the baby.

The fall from the horse and subsequent scare had led Paige to a complete change of heart. Where, previously, she had regarded her pregnancy as a horrible inconvenience, she now wanted this child with every fibre of her being. Today would show her if Luke felt the same.

Not having witnessed an ultrasound scan before, Luke seemed alarmed at first to see the tiny heart beating so fiercely before this gave way to fascination that he really could see a tiny person growing inside Paige – the baby they shared.

'And, as you can see now, you're having a baby girl,' the young woman conducting the scan told them softly, not wanting to intrude on their mood of fascinated absorption at what they could see. Paige, with tears of joy falling unheeded from her eyes, was clinging to Luke's hand.

'Look,' she said. 'Our own little girl – I can't take my eyes off her.'

'That's OK.' The woman smiled at them. 'I can give you some pictures to take away.'

'Now will you promise to marry me?' Luke asked again, as he drove her home, although he knew he had little hope of success. 'At some time in the future, at least?'

'First let us see if Pierette can do well in the Caulfield Cup.'

'Hmm. Are you sure you can trust her to young Glenda? There are some interstate jockeys coming for the carnival and they'll be hungry for rides. And this is a major race.'

'I trust Glenda implicitly. And if she can't take Pierette around, I shall ride her myself.'

'Over my dead—'

'Only joking,' Paige laughed.

CHAPTER TWELVE

Caulfield Cup Day dawned bright and beautiful, the sun rising in a cloudless blue sky with only the slightest breeze to lift the hats and ruffle the new crop of floral summer skirts, many of which were being worn for the first time that day.

Luke had insisted on bringing the whole clan from *Warrender* to enjoy the excitement and carnival atmosphere at first hand that day. Paige was wearing an empire line dress in a cobalt blue with a spray of lily of the valley pinned to her shoulder. Traditionally, this was the flower to be worn on Caulfield Cup Day. Unlike Nanou, who was wearing a full-blown picture hat reminiscent of Gainsborough, she had chosen a small black feather fascinator instead. Luke wore a spray of lily of the valley in the button-hole of his dark-blue suit and, thoughtfully, had provided a spray for Nanou. She pinned it to her wrist in the style of the old-fashioned lady she was, saying that she could both see it and smell it at the same time. The subtle fragrance of the little flowers filled the car, making Marc sneeze and pull a face. Luke had also offered to take Glenda to the track with them but she declined, saying she preferred to ride in the float alongside Gail and the horses.

'It'll feel more like a normal race day,' she said with a shiver, although it was far from cold. 'Keep the jitters at bay.'

'You'll be just fine.' Paige tried to sound reassuring although she could see the girl was a mass of nerves. She could only hope that Glenda would get over them before the big race and not communicate her fears to Pierette.

When they arrived at the course, Marc was delighted to find the redheaded Morgan twins, friends from playschool, already in the members' enclosure along with their parents, Daniel and Foxie, who also had thoroughbred racing stables on the coast although they were not close neighbours. Paige greeted them warmly enough while remaining a little reserved.

'By the way, do you know Luke Sandford?' She drew him forward to be introduced to her friends.

'Only by reputation.' Daniel grinned, shaking him warmly by the hand. 'And as a force to be reckoned with.' His wife smiled, acknowledging the introduction, but she was somewhat distracted, trying to keep an eye on her hyperactive little boys.

'Josh! Joel! Be careful!' she called after them ineffectually as the twins took off without asking permission, jumping on benches and swinging from every available post. Marc followed, giggling, doing his best to keep up with them. 'Why couldn't they have been girls.' Foxie moaned, shaking her head. 'So much easier to manage.'

Luke glanced at Paige and they exchanged a secret smile.

Later, when the Morgans drifted away to greet other friends, Luke had a few questions for Paige. 'Wow,' he said. 'What an extraordinarily beautiful woman.'

'Oh, that's what everyone says when they meet her for

the first time. Someone told me she used to be on TV – an American soap.'

'That explains it. But I sense a little reservation towards them on your part. Why's that?'

'Oh, nothing really and Marc loves to play with her boys. But, as you see, she has no control over them. She lets them run wild and I'm afraid they'll get Marc into trouble along with them.'

'Can't keep him wrapped up in cotton wool, Paige. It's good for him to spend time with his peers. Especially coming from an all female household like yours.'

'Now why did I know you'd say that.'

Excitement was building as it was almost time for the running of the Caulfield Cup. More often than not, the race was run in fine weather and today was no exception. A capacity crowd had turned out to see it and not a single seat remained empty in the stands. Marc returned from the Morgans, pink-cheeked, with a scratch on his leg and a jagged tear in his new shorts but Paige hadn't the heart to scold him.

Following the usual tradition, the riders had come out to be individually introduced to the crowd and Paige was relieved to see that Glenda seemed to have pulled herself together and conquered her nerves. Wearing the Warrender colours of pink with a white diamond and cap, she was nonchalantly tapping her whip against her boot and looking like an old hand.

The National Anthem was sung by a spike-haired pop star in a mini-dress and high heels, whose big voice surprised everyone as it came from such a tiny body. As soon as she finished, the horses began their parade in the mounting yard and very soon the feature race would be under way.

Nanou and Paige went down to meet Glenda and give her last minute instructions while Luke remained in the stands with Marc. Chastened, as he would have to spend the rest of the day in torn pants, the little boy was unusually quiet.

'You know what to do as well as I do, Glenda.' Paige tried to bolster the girl's ego with last minute reassurance. 'Just do as well as you can with the job you know how to do. Remember not to get caught up with horses behind and in front of you, leaving you no way out. In a race like this, you want to dictate your own terms. And you can depend on Pierette to hold something in reserve to give you a good finish. A trick of mine is to hang back and slip through on the inside when they drift away from the rail. She's used to that.'

'Oh, Paige.' Glenda bit her lip. 'I'll do my best to remember it all and try not to let you down.'

'Don't worry,' Paige said, remembering the day she was sick and the mare won the race on her own. 'Pierette will see you through.'

The start of the race was rough. In spite of the stewards' additional warning that they would stand for no jostling or dangerous riding, two of the younger jockeys fought for the same position, collided and fell, causing mayhem for everyone else. Luckily, Glenda, taking note of Paige's instructions, was able to hang back and avoid the disaster. After that early mishap, the race was run almost sedately.

Excitement mounted in the crowd as the horses bunched and then spread out at the home turn, trying to choose the position that suited them most. Glenda, not wanting to go too soon but also afraid of making her move too late, encouraged Pierette to slip through on the inside as the field moved away from the fence.

194

The eyes of everyone seemed to be on the favourite who was now struggling mid field and that included those of the race caller whose attention had not yet been claimed by Pierette. Just as Paige hoped, the mare found an additional burst of speed and bounded to the finishing post, leaving the first and second favourites to be satisfied with gaining only a place.

Gail, sitting with them in the stands, let rip with a shriek that would have startled a demon out of hell, making them all laugh.

'Nanou! Nanou it's happened just like a told you!' Paige hugged her grandmother. 'You just won the Caulfield Cup!'

'To be fair, *chérie*, I'd say that *you* did.'

They all came down from the stands to meet Glenda who seemed to be in a state of shock, unable to believe she had actually won the race.

'I was numb and on automatic pilot the whole time,' she confessed quietly to Paige. 'But Pierette was wonderful – she did it all by herself.'

'That wasn't what I saw,' Paige insisted. 'You played the game just the way I told you and it paid off.'

With the feature race won and the prize-giving over, Luke could see Paige was exhausted and suggested they should go home. Marc, having worn himself out playing with the Morgan twins, was also stifling yawns. Drained by all the excitement, everyone was only too ready to leave.

Although nobody wanted to stay up late celebrating, neither did they want to cook at home, so Luke insisted on buying champagne and Chinese take-away for everyone, including Glenda and Gail. They all sat around the big kitchen table at *Warrender*, Nanou and Paige still dressed in their finery although they'd kicked off their shoes while Glenda and Gail were still in their everyday work clothes.

'What a fantastic team effort.' Luke toasted them. 'Owner, trainer and rider – and don't let's forget the strapper and even the horse – all girls.'

Glenda and Gail excused themselves after the meal – Glenda saying she was ready to sleep the clock around and Gail because she had a date.

Marc was so tired, he let Nanou haul him off to bed without asking Luke for a story. The old lady didn't return, leaving Paige and Luke at the kitchen table alone.

Luke leaned over it to cover Paige's hand with his own.

'I need to ask you something. Are you ready to marry me now you're a rich woman in your own right?'

Paige sighed and smiled at him, knowing he was going to keep asking until she agreed. 'Yes, Luke, I will marry you. But not until after our baby is born.'

'OK,' he said, stroking the back of her hand with his thumb. 'If that's the way you want it. I'd just like to understand why.'

She thought for a moment before replying. 'Because I never had a proper wedding with Ruary. I missed out on all the festivities and didn't even have time to buy a new dress. And it was so furtive and rushed. Just five minutes before some marriage celebrant who was a friend of a friend, followed by a scrap of paper informing me that I was now Mrs Ruary McHugh. I didn't even feel married and it didn't take us long to realize we had made a dreadful mistake. This time I want a wedding day to remember as well as a film and pictures we can look at again and again. And I certainly don't want to get married with a lump hiding behind a big bunch of flowers. So it has to be after the baby is born.'

He turned her hand over and kissed her palm, sending shivers down her spine. Pregnant or not, she still loved and wanted him and it was hard on both of them, having to wait. Since Paige's fall and the scare over losing the baby, they had been wary of making love.

'All right,' he said at last, taking a small black velvet box from his pocket. 'But I hope you won't object to being officially engaged?'

Paige waited as he took a box from his pocket and opened it, showing her a beautiful antique ring, lying inside – a large emerald, surrounded by a cluster of diamonds.

'Oh, Luke, it's so beautiful,' she whispered.

'It belonged to Celia, my mother. It's a family heirloom. I had it cleaned and reset.'

'Celia – was that her name? I like that. Very Shakespearean.'

'I told you we came from the bard's old stamping ground.'

'Why not call our own little girl Celia, too?'

'I'd love it, of course, but what about Nanou? D'you think she'll be offended if we don't call the baby Paige?'

'We can't have three Paiges all in the same house, that would be too confusing. But there's nothing wrong with giving it as a second name.'

'Celia Paige – it has a nice ring to it.' He frowned at her with mock severity. 'But you have to be quite sure this is what you want. There's no going back once I've announced our engagement in the paper.'

'Not a chance.' She examined her hand with the new ring on her finger and gave him a mischievous smile. 'I love this beautiful ring and I won't give it back.'

He put his hands on either side of her face and kissed her with tenderness and care as if she were the most fragile and precious thing in the world.

She slapped him playfully. 'Oh, for goodness' sake, Luke. I'm not made of glass.' She stood up and came into his arms, pulling him close. 'Now give me a proper kiss to celebrate our engagement. With a sigh of happiness, he complied.

Most people were delighted to hear of their engagement, quick to send gifts and messages. People might be beginning to suspect about the baby but no one said anything. Paige was still slender and only those who knew her well could recognize subtle changes. Inundated with cards and e-mails, she answered all of them, even the ones from people she didn't know.

She had never felt happier or more settled in the whole of her life. Her only regret was concerning Pierette. Instead of going on from her victory at Caulfield to compete in the prestigious Cox Plate or the Melbourne Cup, the mare had pulled up very sore. Although the vet didn't think there was a tear in the tendon, there was heat and inflammation and the mare would have to rest, postponing her campaign until the following year.

And, one morning, on arrival at Sunny Orchards too late for track work as usual, Paige witnessed a little scene playing out between Luke and Gail.

'Uh-oh,' Gail said, noting his grim expression. 'Not another one?'

'Yep,' Luke said as he screwed it into a ball and thrust it into his pocket, hiding it from view. 'Hotting up, too. Third one this week.'

'Third what?' said Paige, picking up on their less than happy expressions.

Not having seen her approach, they both started guiltily. 'Nothing!' they said in unison.

'Oh, come on.' Paige glanced from one to the other, seeing their wary expressions. 'I know you both better than that. You're hiding something, aren't you?'

'Nothing that need worry you.' Luke gave Gail a sharp look, warning her to keep silent.

'Right.' Paige plonked herself down on a bench outside the stables and folded her arms. 'Suit yourselves but I'm not shifting from here till I know what it is.'

'Might as well tell her, Luke.' Gail gave him a friendly clap on the shoulder. 'She'll keep on at you till you do.' With a rueful smile she hefted some tack on to her shoulder and disappeared into the stables to clean it and hang it up, leaving Luke to deal with Paige on his own.

'So what terrible secret are you hiding that Gail knows?' she teased. 'You've got another girl friend in Queensland who's expecting you to marry her instead of me?'

Luke smiled but she could see it was strained. 'Nothing like that,' he said. 'OK. I'm getting notes from Sarah Canning – Julia's sister. She sends at least one a week – wishing us ill.'

'But you're not taking her seriously, are you?' She could sense his reluctance to say more. 'Come on, Luke, you can't tell just half the tale. I need to know what's going on.'

'The earlier ones were just rants – you know the sort of thing – she wished I was dead and buried and her sister alive. But this last week she's changed her tune to include you, too. I don't know what will happen when she finds out about the baby – as she undoubtedly will.'

Paige thought for a moment before speaking. 'After the funeral, did you ever set her straight about Julia? Did you tell her about all those terrible things she did to us? I'll bet you didn't even mention the stabbing at the restaurant?'

'What would have been the point? I wanted to leave Sarah with only the best memories of her sister. I saw no reason to hurt her by telling her what a crazy bitch Julia really was.'

'So now she sees us as the bad guys while her sister remains a saint?'

'I suppose so.' He shrugged.

'Can I see her letters?'

'No way. I destroyed them all as soon as I got them.'

'They were evidence, Luke. Without them you have no proof. Just show me the last one then.'

'No, Paige. It'll only upset you,' he said, although she continued to hold out her hand until reluctantly he produced the crumpled ball of paper and let her smooth out the creases to read it.

Although she didn't expect it, on reading the angry words Sarah had written, almost stabbing a hole in the paper, Paige found that she was indeed upset.

Marry Paige Warrender, Luke, and you'll live to regret it. Lose all hope of leading a happy and peaceful life. Every bad deed in this world is repaid so expect to reap a reward for your treachery. Keep watch because you'll never know how or when I will strike. You should suffer the blackest misery for the way you treated my sister – you and Paige both. Believe me when I say I will never give up and never forget. I am always on your case. Sarah C.

Paige finished reading and looked up at him with tears in her eyes.

'There you go,' he said, shaking his head. 'I told you not to read it.'

'But she has to be stopped. We must see a solicitor – get a restraining order. We can't live with this constant threat hanging over us.'

'If we don't rise to the bait, she'll get tired of it in time and give up.'

'I wouldn't count on it. I know Sarah better than that. I was at school with her, remember? She's nothing if not tenacious. As she says – she'll never give up and never forget. There's only one way out: I'll have to see her.'

'Indeed you will not.' Luke stared at her, appalled. 'She sounds almost as crazy as Julia. And you're pregnant, she might—'

'She won't do me a physical injury – that's not her style. And like all bullies, she's a coward at heart.'

'Then I'm going with you. You're not going to see her alone.'

'I have to. You'd be like a red rag to a bull. But if you must come, you can wait for me outside in the car. I'll have my mobile phone.'

'Which will be completely useless if Sarah knocks you on the head and locks you up in the basement.'

Paige had to laugh at this. 'What an imagination you have.'

'You didn't see the look on Julia's face when she stabbed me. Like a female devil.'

When Paige rang the doorbell at Sarah's home that afternoon, Westminster chimes echoed somewhere deep in the house. For just a moment, her courage failed her and she began to hope no one was home. But after a moment she heard slippers shuffling across the marble tiles of the hall. The front door was yanked open upon although the security grille remained in place. Paige knew someone was there on the other side but she couldn't see through it.

'Hello?' she said tentatively. 'Sarah is that you?'

'Go away, Paige.' The woman's voice came out as a low growl. 'I don't want to speak to you.'

'I'm afraid you have no choice. You've opened a whole can of worms here, Sarah, and I won't leave until we've settled things once and for all.'

'I got to him, didn't I?' There was a short mirthless laugh. 'You, too. Good.'

'Sarah, we have to talk because there are certain things I need to tell you about Julia. Things you don't know.'

'Nothing you have to say can hurt Julia now. She's dead.'

'I know and I'm sorry. I know how much she meant to you.'

'I can see where you're coming from, Paige. You've come to plead with me because you believe in my curse.'

'Curses have a life of their own, Sarah they have a nasty habit of rebounding on the people who made them. The only person you'll really hurt is yourself.'

Paige heard a snort of disgust and sensed that her one-time friend was about to close the door, cutting short any further communication. 'OK, slam the door in my face if you like, and hide from the truth. But there's a lot about your sister that you need to know.' And she waited, holding her breath, hoping she had piqued Sarah's curiosity.

There was a sigh of resignation as the security door was clicked open and Sarah stood aside, indicating that she should come in. 'I'll give you five minutes,' she said, glancing at her watch.

'Make it ten.' Paige's confidence was growing by the minute. Her mental image of Sarah had been the well-groomed high school princess of her memory. Although she had come here without warning, it was a surprise to find her old schoolfriend wearing a grubby tracksuit and bedroom slippers, her fair hair dull and unwashed, hanging in her eyes. She saw also that Sarah was pregnant and guessed that she was about a month in advance of herself.

'You're having a baby,' she blurted, without meaning to as Sarah led the way to the kitchen. Such a social pariah as herself was not to be invited into the drawing-room.

'Yes, I am.' The girl gave her a sharp look over her shoulder. 'Not that it's any business of yours. Simon and I are having a son.'

'You'll like that,' Paige said, receiving a grunt for an answer.

On reaching the kitchen, Sarah put a kettle on and reached into a cupboard for mugs. 'Tea?'

'Thank you. Long as it isn't laced with hemlock.'

'Now why didn't I think of that?' Sarah narrowed her eyes, a mannerism she often affected, reminding Paige all too vividly of the time that they had been friends at school.

Sarah plonked a kitchen mug in front of her with a tea-bag afloat in it Clearly her unwelcome visitor was not to be offered the best china. 'You have six minutes left and you're out of here. Better get on with it.'

Paige drew a deep breath, praying for fluency. Although she knew the truth about Julia was bound to be hurtful, there was no point in pulling her punches and Sarah must be convinced she was telling the truth. She told her stories concisely and without dramatizing any emotion. Just the facts and without any hint of criticism. By the time she starting talking of Marc and his kidnapping, Sarah was breathing heavily, her arms folded across her chest as if holding her anger in place.

'How dare you come here with your lies,' she whispered. 'And as for kidnapping your son – I never heard anything so ridiculous. Julia doesn't – didn't even like children. How can you sit there, telling such lies about a woman who's no longer here to defend herself? You just want to make yourself feel better about stealing her man.'

Paige shook her head. 'Sarah, I know this is hard but—'

'Hard? You can't begin to know how I feel. I've lost my sister – my wonderful sister who was the world to me.' Chest heaving, Sarah could scarcely speak, her face crumpling into a mask of misery. 'Get out of here now. Get out of my house.'

'Not until you've heard all I have to say.' Paige reached across the table for Sarah's hand, only to have it snatched away. 'Luke didn't want me to tell you this, even now. He wanted to leave your memories intact.'

'So why can't you?' Sarah stood up and reached into a cupboard for a box of tissues, grabbed a handful and noisily blew her nose.

'Because there is more,' Paige continued gently. 'But I'll leave if you don't want to hear it. I think my ten minutes are up.'

Sarah let out a long breath, finally willing to listen. 'That doesn't matter now.' She was speaking through a blocked nose, sounding as if she had a cold. 'Have another cup of tea and tell me the rest of it. There's no point in hanging back now.'

And she listened, wide-eyed, her hands covering her mouth, as Paige went on to tell her about the night of Julia's death and how she had thrust a knife through Luke's hand, pinning him to the table.

'She wouldn't,' she whispered through her fingers, shaking her head. 'Julia couldn't do that.'

'I'm afraid she did. If you don't believe me, you can go to the restaurant and ask them yourself. The manager drove Luke to the hospital to get his hand stitched.'

Sarah flinched, still shaking her head. 'So why didn't he tell me? Explain what happened that night?'

'Did you give him the chance?'

204

Sarah didn't answer but wiped away more tears.

'Sarah, I promise that everything I've told you is the truth. But I'll quite understand if you don't want to believe it.'

'Unfortunately, I'm beginning to.' Sarah blew her nose again before going on, 'I meant all those nice things I said about Julia at her funeral because I wanted, no, I *needed* everyone to think well of her. It was the only thing I had left to do for her. Because, most of the time, she was wonderful, just like I said. She raised me after our mother died, put me through college and even introduced me to Simon who was a client of hers. But, like a counter-balance, Julia also had a dark side. It didn't happen often but she had a cruel temper that terrified me when I was small. I didn't want to remember it but there was a time – I was scarcely into my teens – when I borrowed a necklace from her box without asking and I lost it. It wasn't valuable – just costume jewellery – but she flew into a rage and slapped my face so hard I fell down. Then she found a hammer, went upstairs to my room and destroyed my whole collection of little glass animals. I tried to stop her but there were splinters of glass going everywhere and some went into my hands. I was in pain, screaming and begging her to stop, but it was as if she was in another place, another time and couldn't hear me. She seemed almost surprised when she came out of it and saw the blood on my hands.'

There was a silence between them then as if neither knew what to say next until Sarah continued in a low voice, lacing her hands to cradle her coming child, 'I wouldn't have been able to leave my baby alone with her – not ever. I'd never be certain of her temper or what she might do.'

Paige shivered, wondering what might have happened if

Marc had angered Julia during that long afternoon they had spent together. 'I am so sorry for you,' she said at last. 'Sorry for the loss of your sister. But now I want nothing more than to know that it's over. I want your promise that there will be no more letters or threats to me or to Luke.'

Sarah bit her lip. 'I feel dreadful about that now. I was so vile to him and he never said a word. And you're pregnant, too. When is the baby due?'

'Some time in February. Round about the same time as yours.'

'Paige,' she began hesitantly, 'do you think . . . is it possible for us to be friends again?'

'Now, Sarah, what do you want with me?' Paige giggled, lightening the mood. 'The popular high school princess wanting to be friends with the stable girl?'

'I was only popular because of all those free tickets from Julia. You were always the glamorous one with your French grandmother and your horses.'

Paige laughed then without inhibition. 'Sarah, I can honestly say I've never been glamorous in the whole of my life. But yes, I think we can be friends again. After all, we're having babies at around the same time. They might even grow up to be friends.' This time it was Paige who glanced at her watch, wide-eyed. 'Wow, look at the time. The ten minutes you gave me have stretched into almost an hour. Luke will be thinking you really have knocked me on the head and locked me in the basement.' This made them both laugh.

CHAPTER THIRTEEN

Paige's daughter, Celia Paige, was born in the small, local hospital in the middle of a hot afternoon in February. Her delivery had been speedy and almost painless with Luke present, emotionally exhausted and rendered almost speechless by witnessing the miracle of birth at first hand. He seemed totally enthralled by their tiny daughter, unable to take his eyes off the baby girl and making Nanou smile.

In the next room lay Sarah who hadn't been quite so fortunate. Due to complications during a long and overdue labour, her little boy had been born by Caesarian section and, at one time, the doctors thought of sending him to the Children's Hospital to make sure he survived. But, happily, the little boy had proved to be stronger than they expected and was now doing well although Sarah remained depressed and fearful. Simon, her fiancé a man of few words, was doing his best to comfort her but without success. Paige also did her best to cheer her old friend.

'Just look at him.' She studied the baby in Sarah's arms. 'Going from strength to strength. You'll be taking him home soon.'

'Ooh, not yet,' Sarah continued to wail. 'I haven't found a nanny and I'll never manage without one. And everything seems to hurt – even trying to feed him.'

'It gets better, I promise.' Paige sat on the side of the bed, hugging the girl's thin shoulders. 'Your milk is the best possible food for little Eliot as well as a good way of getting your figure back. Don't you feel the muscles contracting when you feed him?'

'Hmm.' Sarah's humour was grim. 'Do you think he was born with teeth? Because that's what it feels like.'

In the end Paige had to give up and leave. She would try again with Sarah later but right now she didn't want her friend's gloom to affect her own happy mood.

Back in her own room, Nanou held the precious bundle that was Celia, wrapped in a pale pink shawl she had knitted herself, smiling down at her great-granddaughter with tears of happiness standing in her eyes, her heart full. For once she had nothing to say.

Marc was the only one who seemed disappointed in Celia, peering at the tiny bundle with deep suspicion.

'Are you sure that's our baby?' he whispered to his mother at last. 'It's very small and very red, isn't it?'

'Not it. She,' Paige corrected.

'Well, she doesn't look like anyone I know. When is she going to open her eyes and talk to me?'

'You'll have to be patient,' Paige said softly, leaning over to give him a kiss and ruffle his hair. 'It takes a very long time for babies to walk and talk.'

Marc sighed, bored with the infant's overpowering need to sleep. Luke offered to take him to look at the small lake in the hospital grounds. There were ducks there, always hopeful of getting a snack.

Although Nanou would have raised no objections, Luke preferred not to move into *Warrender* until after the wedding. It was planned to take place in late April before winter could really set in. To help Paige recover her former level of fitness, he arranged for a new swimming pool to be installed at Sunny Orchards, and converted one of the front rooms into a small gym, complete with light weights and exercise machines. It was an early wedding present, he said. Paige was delighted but insisted that Luke's other apprentices, together with Glenda and Gail, should be allowed to use these facilities, too.

'I'll work harder at the swimming if I have competition,' She assured him. 'I'm not sure I'll be able to get back to riding on race day but I'd like to be fit enough to work with the horses at home.'

Luke had also offered to engage a nanny to look after Celia and Marc, but Nanou wouldn't hear of it.

'Why should you pay some girl to come here while I sit twiddling my thumbs?' she grumbled.

'I thought you'd have enough to do, looking after your roses?' Luke smiled at her. He had presented Nanou with two dozen fragrant Delbard French roses to replace the old bushes ruined by vandals. They would make a good show the following spring as she now had twice as many as she had before.

'Once they're established in the ground and trimmed, Luke, there'll be nothing for me to do till they start to shoot. Celia will be more active at that time – we can talk about getting a nanny then.'

Luke smiled, knowing very well that she wouldn't.

Paige, frugal in most aspects of her life, had her heart set on an elaborate wedding. There would be a marquee in one of the paddocks at *Warrender*, an almost famous wedding celebrant had been engaged and for once no expense was to be spared. To please Nanou, Paige would have married in church but, since Luke was divorced, they all agreed that a less formal ceremony would be more appropriate.

All the same, Nanou was to have a new outfit and play the *grand dame* of *Warrender* and Paige insisted that Luke was to dress up in the morning suit he had once worn to Ascot.

'Oh no, Paige,' he groaned. 'Not the top hat and grey tails? I don't even know if I can still get into it and I'll feel as if I'm appearing in *My Fair Lady*.'

'I don't care. You can starve yourself into it,' she said, for once in her life determined to play the princess and have her own way. She also rounded up Glenda and Gail, asking them to be her attendants. Expecting an enthusiastic response, she was taken aback when the twins received this invitation with obvious mixed feelings.

'What's the matter now?' she said, seeing their glum expressions. 'I thought you'd be pleased.'

The twins exchanged glances and then Glenda spoke up for both of them. 'It all depends on what you want us to wear. You see, we've been through all this before. People like having identical twin bridesmaids to appear like book-ends on either side of the bride but we had a bad experience a couple of years ago. Our cousin wanted us to wear the most awful dresses in a bilious green, the colour of cat sick. We refused and it ended badly with lost friendships and hurt feelings all round.'

Paige laughed. 'I won't ask you to wear bile or any other green. Some racing people think it's an unlucky colour. Better still, you can come with me to the bridal shop – then you can choose for yourselves and help me with mine.'

'Great,' the twins said in unison. 'You're on.'

It took a long time for the three girls to find the right

dress for Paige. Petite as she was, a dress with a hooped underskirt made her look like a tea-cosy doll and heavy lace swamped her, hiding the figure it had taken no little effort to regain. Finally, they discovered a dress reminiscent of Cinderella's ball gown in heavy, white satin. Sleeveless, it had a scooped neckline and was fitted as far as the hips before widening into a generous A line skirt. A sash of rich cream satin made an apron effect in front with a soft bow behind – a detail for people to look at while the couple were saying their vows. Having chosen the dress, Paige's next choice would have been a head-dress of artificial orange blossoms attached to an enormous froth of a veil which would trail behind her but the twins firmly advised her against it.

'I know the smaller one's not as spectacular,' Gail went on to explain, 'but you'll manage it better. We saw a wedding once when it took the bridegroom a good five minutes to find his way through the veil to kiss the bride. And you'll have to take it off, anyway, if you want to dance.'

'You seem to know your way around this,' Paige said. 'You've been to a lot of weddings.'

'You can say that again.' Gail smiled. 'We come from a very large family. We've attended the weddings of two older sisters and five cousins – all girls.'

Having found the right dress for Paige, the twins set about finding something suitable for themselves. Waiting outside their changing room, Paige could hear a lot of giggling until they emerged dressed in identical dresses of gauzy, electric pink, looking like a pair of Christmas fairies. All they lacked was a pair of sparkling wings. Paige bit her lip, wondering what to say. She *had* promised that they could choose for themselves.

'Tarahh!' Gail sang out, twirling around.

'Gorgeous, don't you think?' Glenda said, fluttering her eyelashes.

'But – this is almost as bad as bile green,' Paige said through gritted teeth, trying not to let them see she was getting upset.

'Only joking' Glenda said. 'You should see your face. Don't worry, we've picked out a nice little number in lilac to complement your own.'

Five minutes later, Paige sighed with relief when she saw this was true. The twins had chosen identical strapless pale lilac gowns in a heavy satin, to be worn with matching elbow-length gloves, hiding hands that were more than a little work-worn due to their daily contact with horses, saddles and tack. With their prizes duly ordered, they rode back from Melbourne in Paige's old car, singing happily along to old country tunes on the radio. Paige cringed as the twins yodelled like cowhands, knowing how much she detested it.

On her wedding day, Paige was up early as usual, anxious to see what kind of weather Melbourne was going to serve up for her special day. She opened her bedroom window to watch the sun rise in a sky the colour of rose pearl, peppered with just a few scudding clouds. A light breeze blew across from the sea, just sufficient to rustle the leaves on the trees and make her shiver in anticipation. She breathed a sigh of contentment, silently thanking the gods for this perfect day.

Gail and Glenda had stayed overnight at *Warrender*, anxious to make themselves useful. Marc was up early, delighted to find the girls staying in his house, rampaging from room to room until Nanou warned him to stop getting over-excited and let everyone get dressed. The wedding was

212

to take place at two in the afternoon with a high tea to follow. Right now it might seem that there was plenty of time but all that could change. The twins had taken charge of Nanou and transformed her usual neat but severe French pleat into an enormous, silver 'cottage loaf' that softened and flattered her features. She had chosen a beautiful smoke-blue dress with a matching coat which everyone said made her look like a duchess.

Celia, at just over two months of age, was a placid and happy child with a smile for everyone. Even Marc had now fallen under her spell. Paige was still feeding the child herself and didn't want to stop – even for the sake of an uninterrupted honeymoon – so they would be taking her with them to Merimbula. Marc found it hard to grasp the concept that Celia would be going with them on their honeymoon while he must be left behind.

'But why do you have to go to the moon and eat honey?' he frowned. 'It's a long way for you to go without me an' Nanou.'

'A honeymoon isn't exactly that,' Paige tried to explain. 'It's a holiday for people who just got married.'

'Well, I'd like to go on a holiday, too. So would Nanou.'

'It's just for a little while. We'll be back before you know it.'

'That's what you said when you went to Sydney last year,' the little boy grumbled. 'You took long enough then.' Still sulking, he pulled a long face at the page-boy's outfit Nanou had sewn for him – a blue velvet coat and breeches with long white socks and black patent shoes. 'Do I really have to wear that?'

'Yes, you do.' Paige was suddenly out of patience. 'It's a great honour for you to be our page-boy and ring-bearer you know. Quite a responsibility.' She pretended to give it some thought for a moment. 'But of course – if you don't want to do it, we can always ask somebody else.'

'Who?' The little boy seized the costume, crushing it against his chest. 'They'll have to fight me for it first!'

The wedding was all Paige had ever hoped for and more. The best man was Robin Wilkes, an old friend of Luke's from Hong Kong who had flown in specially for the occasion just two days before. Although his acquaintance with Paige was brief, in addition to toasting the bridesmaids, he managed to give an amusing and complimentary speech about the bride and groom. In addition, he was a flawless MC, doing much to keep everything going smoothly. A man in his late thirties, fair-haired, with designer stubble and an elegant moustache, he was good-looking enough to cause instant rivalry between the twins. All afternoon he flirted shamelessly with them until they were almost ready to come to blows. And when he left them, briefly, to speak to Nanou, Glenda tackled her sister.

'Back off, Gail, you're being unfair. You've already got a boyfriend.'

'Exactly. Just a boyfriend. Nothing at all like him.' Gail gave Robin a smouldering glance from across the room. 'He's the genuine article. A real man.'

'It's not fair. If you'd just take yourself off for five minutes, I know he'd—'

'What seems to be the trouble, girls?' It was Luke who spoke. While they had been quarrelling, he had come up behind them. 'Not fighting over Robin, I hope?'

They scowled at each other but said nothing, waiting to hear what Luke had to say.

He didn't speak until they'd stopped glaring at each other and gave him their full attention. 'Because you'll be wasting your time if you are.'

'What do you mean?' said Gail. 'Is he married or something?'

'No, but he certainly isn't single. He has a partner in Hong Kong and they've been together for years. Robin's gay.'

'He can't be,' Glenda said. 'Look at him. He's been flirting with us all day and now he's teasing Nanou – she's gone all pink.'

'She can handle it.' Luke poured them each another glass of champagne. 'Sorry, but that's what he does. Safety in numbers you know.'

'Ooh.' Gail's shoulders slumped. 'Wharrashame.'

'So I don't want to see you two girls falling out over *him*.' Luke put an arm around each of them. 'Drink up and be happy. It's my wedding day.'

Paige was due for another surprise when she came downstairs dressed in a new but casual tracksuit ready for travel. They had decided to honeymoon in Merimbula and although they would start the journey that night, they wouldn't actually get there until the end of the following day. Expecting that they would be taking Luke's silver Porsche which had already been tastefully decorated for them with tin cans, toilet paper and lurid balloons, Paige was surprised when he threw their cases into the sleek looking silver wagon beside it instead.

'It's for you.' He gave her a swift kiss and a hug. 'Happy wedding day, Paige. With two kids to ferry around, you'll need something reliable.'

'But you already gave me a wonderful wedding present – the swimming pool and the gym.'

'Which you insisted on sharing with everyone else. This

present is just for you. I've already had it a month and it's nicely run in.'

'I don't know what to say. I feel terrible because I don't have anything more to give you.'

'You've already given me Celia – the daughter I never expected to have. And you let me share Marc. I look forward to helping you raise your son.'

Paige leaned in and allowed herself to be subjected to a long and lingering kiss until it was interrupted with shouts of glee and a hail of confetti from their wedding guests and most of the hands from Sunny Orchards. Only Ham Peachey had refused to be present, grumbling that with all these strangers wandering all over the place, someone had to stay sober and keep an eye on the horses.

The back seat of the wagon had been fitted with a belt to restrain Celia's bassinet and, as usual, having been fed when Paige went upstairs to change out of her wedding dress, the baby was sleeping peacefully. But now it was time to leave.

Luke shook Robin's hand and gave him a hug. 'Thank you so much for coming to Melbourne,' he said. 'It wouldn't have gone half so well without you.'

'My pleasure,' he replied. 'Wouldn't have missed it for anything.'

Paige also hugged Luke's friend and thanked him as well before turning to Nanou who was standing there, lost in admiration of Paige's new wheels.

'Thank you for everything,' she said to her grandmother. 'Not just for today – all those years—'

'Hush,' the old lady said. 'There's no need for that. You'll have me in tears.'

'Oh, Nanou, I love you so much,' Paige said, tears of sentiment standing in her own eyes.

216

Luke also embraced the old lady and then it was time for the difficult task of saying goodbye to Marc.

'Want to go with you, too,' he whispered, close to tears, still dressed in the Blue Boy suit that he hated.

'Come on, Marc,' Gail said, trying to distract him. 'I'm starved. Let's go and find some ice cream—'

Unusually bad-tempered, he shook her off. 'Don't want ice cream,' he yelled at last. 'I want to go with Mummy and Luke.'

Stricken, Paige half turned towards him until Nanou signalled for them to get in the car and go. Gail swept the little boy up into a firm embrace, strong enough to hold him although he was fighting her all the while and starting to cry.

CHAPTER FOURTEEN

The house at Merimbula was even lovelier than Paige remembered it. Although Luke had not allowed the real estate agents to lease it, he had enlisted their help in finding a cleaning service and gardening service as well as arranging with a local firm selling white goods to refurnish the laundry, replacing his mother's old-fashioned washing-machine and ancient fridge. He had even had the foresight to include a drier.

She discovered also a new bed, made up with new linen in the room they had shared before. A cradle had been added with mosquito netting for Celia. The double bed in his mother's old room had been replaced with two king singles instead. In the living area, a comfortable, modern lounge suite had been installed, replacing his mother's shabby old sofa and chairs. Even the old television set was gone, replaced by a new plasma attached to the wall. Paige didn't remark on it but she could see that Luke wanted nothing left to remind her of any negatives from the time she was here before. Only the kitchen and dining settings had been allowed to remain. New outside blinds had been added to shield the rooms from the afternoon sun and new curtains decorated the windows.

'Luke, it's beautiful,' she whispered, as she walked from room to room holding Celia close. 'But you must have spent a small fortune getting it done.'

'Why not?' he said. 'We're going to be spending most of our holidays and long weelends up here after all. But if there's anything you don't like – or want to change – you have only to say.'

'No, no. I love it just as it is,' she said. 'You've made it into a magical corner of the world.'

'It was always that.' He smiled, gathering both wife and baby into his arms. 'It just needed the right person to see it, that's all.'

In spite of Luke's protests that they could eat out, Paige once more insisted on going around the local supermarket for supplies while he followed her, grumbling and shaking his head. The girl who served them seemed to remember them from their previous visit, casting admiring glances at Celia who responded at once, beaming at her.

'My but she's a pretty one.' The girl cocked her head and gave them a knowing, sideways smile. 'A real love child.'

'She's certainly that.' Luke picked up their bag of groceries. 'Everyone loves our Celia.'

'See you again.' The girl gave them a brief wave and went to spread the news of Luke's arrival with his wife and new baby.

Much later, after a simple supper of the local oysters and cooked prawns tossed in a salad, they went to bed. Paige wore a black lace nightgown for the occasion which had cost her almost as much as she would expect to pay for an evening dress. Luke's reaction was worth it as he lay watching her, hands linked behind his head when she came in from the bathroom.

'Oh, wow!' he said softly. 'What did I ever do to deserve this?' And, as she drew closer, the familiar smell of *Black Orchid* reached his nostrils. 'Don't tell me you still have it, after all this time?'

'No. I had to buy a new one. I kept the old one too long and it went off.'

'There!' he said. 'I told you it was to splash around.'

She climbed on to the bed and crawled towards him until she was suspended over him, leaning on her hands. Their kiss was long, unhurried and satisfying although the love-making that followed was cautious at first; this was the first time they had indulged themselves since Celia's birth and Luke was too nervous to do so with complete abandon, for fear of hurting her.

'Luke, it's all right,' she said at last. 'I won't break.'

'I can't remember you being this small and fragile,' he said. 'You were always so sturdy before.'

'Oh, do come on,' she whispered, nipping his ear. 'Or I'll think you've gone off me.'

'There is absolutely no chance of that.' He gathered her into a tight embrace, making her gasp with pleasure. 'But take off this beautiful garment first or I'm in danger of tearing it.'

She sat back on her heels to do so, allowing him to admire her breasts, unusually voluptuous and ready for the business of feeding Celia. He cupped them gently as if afraid to squeeze them, making Paige sigh with the comfortable familiarity of it.

'I'd forgotten how beautiful you are,' he said, making her smile.

Savouring the moment, she was about to ease herself on to his member again when a strident cry from the cradle froze them both. Temporarily, they had forgotten their daughter.

'What now?' Paige got up and pulled on a dressing gown 'As a rule she never wakes up when I've settled her for the night.'

'It happens,' Luke said. 'The house is strange to her.'

'She probably just needs to know that we're here. I'll give her a small feed and she'll go back to sleep.' Paige settled herself with Celia in the big bedroom chair and offered the baby her breast. The child's eager mouth closed around it and she began sucking vigorously. Luke propped himself on one elbow to watch.

'Look at that,' he said. 'It's something I love to see although I have to say it makes me feel a bit envious.'

'Oh!' Paige said. 'I can go in the other room, if you'd rather.'

'You stay right where you are.' He grinned. 'I'm enjoying this far too much.'

In the morning they took Celia for a long walk along the beach. It was windy and invigorating but not really the weather for swimming. Pelicans flew lazily on the currents and sometimes landing ahead of them on the beach. Under a sunny sky, the water was blue as ever, these beaches well named The Sapphire Coast.

Luke picked up unusual shells to show her and Celia clutched a large one in her tiny hand. Paige took it away when she looked like conveying it to her mouth. But, after a while, Luke observed that his wife was unusually quiet, almost sad and with tears standing in her eyes.

'Tell me what's wrong,' he said, turning her almost roughly towards him. 'I won't have any sadness, any regret. I want this to be the most perfect time for both of us. A golden moment in our lives.'

'And so it is. I was just thinking of Marc. He would love

it so much here. The pelicans. And he just loves collecting shells. And you – you'd be able to teach him to fish.'

'Right,' he said, letting her go so suddenly, she almost stumbled. Without another word he started jogging up the beach on his way back to the house.

Miserably, pushing the pram awkwardly through the drier sand at the top of the beach, Paige followed. *Oh God, he's offended,* she thought. *And I've ruined everything for him. What a prize idiot I am!*

But she was surprised to find Luke in a buoyant mood when she came back to the house with Celia. He poured her a refreshing drink of apple cider and made no mention of the incident on the beach. She didn't mention it either, thinking it best forgotten.

That evening they went to dinner at Tim Foster's restaurant, having his special crayfish again and hoping that Celia would sleep soundly enough not to interrupt their meal.

They weren't interrupted by Celia but by the insistent ringing of Luke's mobile, giving Paige an unpleasant sense of *déjà vu.*

'Sorry, Paige, have to take this,' he mumbled, not just turning away this time but actually walking outside on to the restaurant deck with the phone.

'Anything wrong?' she said when he came back, trying to sound as if it wasn't important.

'Not at all.' He leaned down to drop a kiss on her head before sitting down. 'Just firming up a few details.'

'I thought you were taking a holiday from your businesses while we were here.' She tried to stare at him through the large bunch of flowers that decorated Tim's table.

'Well,' he sighed, 'you know I can't rely on that Wendy. If

only Lucy hadn't gone to America. . . .'

Paige sighed inwardly, too. Somehow she didn't believe he was telling the truth.

The following afternoon, Paige fell asleep in front of the television. She had discovered that feeding and looking after a baby was surprisingly time-consuming and tiring. An hour later she was woken by a car drawing into the driveway of the house and started to her feet.

'Visitors?' she said. 'Not expecting anyone, are we? Who can it be?' Followed by Luke, she went to the front door and opened it just in time to see two uniformed limo drivers lifting luggage out of the boot of the car.

'Excuse me,' she called out to them. Barefooted, she didn't want to venture out on to the gravel. 'But I think you've come to the wrong house.'

The older man grinned, shaking his head, and then a familiar voice hailed her, 'Mummee!'

For a moment she blinked, thinking her ears had deceived her until Marc tumbled out of the car and came running towards her. She caught him in a tight embrace, burying her face in his hair and breathing the all too familiar scent of her own little boy. 'Darling, how lovely. But what are you doing here?'

'We kept going all through the night to get here. That's why we have two drivers,' he said, wriggling. 'Put me down, I want to see everything. We've come to eat honey on your moon.'

'We?' Paige said.

'Oh, yes. Nanou is here, too. She'll come out in a minute. She says she gets stiff after sitting too long.' And, as if on cue, the old lady stepped out of the car, stretching her aching limbs.

'OK, then.' Luke put an arm around Paige's shoulders.

'Did I do right?'

'Oh yes, yes. Everything's perfect now.'

'Perfect?' Nanou almost snorted. 'I never heard anything like it in all of my life. Taking children an' old ladies on a honeymoon. What do you always say? A recipe for disaster.'

'Come in.' Paige kissed her grandmother and urged her inside. 'I want you to see the house. The bad news is that you'll be sharing a room with Marc.'

'Ah well,' Nanou sighed theatrically. 'I suppose there are some sacrifices to be made.'